# THE

## DEVIL'S

# BOARD

# L. Sydney Fisher

**Legacy Books Unlimited, Inc.**

# BOOKS BY L. SYDNEY FISHER

## STANDALONES
*See No Evil*
*The Devil's Board*

## The Phoenix Series
*The Phoenix Mission, Part I*
*The Phoenix Codes, Part II*

## The Bradford Series
*The Haunting of Natalie Bradford, Part I*
*The Haunting of Natalie Bradford, Part II:*
*Waking the Dead*
*The Haunted Prophecy of Natalie Bradford:*
*The Complete Bradford Series*

## The Haunted
*The Haunted: A Haunted History Series,*
*Volume I*
*The Haunted: A Haunted History Series,*
*Volume II*

Published by Legacy Books Unlimited, Inc.

Editing provided by: Independent Editing Services

ISBN-13: 978-0-9991440-1-5

Cover Design: L. Sydney Fisher

*For—*

*Rachel, Nate, Josie, & Spencer*

## A note from the author...

While doing research for *The Devil's Board*, I was contacted by two different individuals who did not know each other and who did not attend Riverside at the same time. Both of these individuals told me about personal experiences they had while a student at Riverside. To my amazement, one of the individuals revealed that they had lived in the very same dorm room where Amber Simmons used the Ouija board in 1987. This person disclosed that they had experienced unexplainable mood swings and depression while living in the room, but they had no knowledge of what had transpired there four years before. And both of the people who contacted me told me that they had paid a visit to Sister Elizabeth Williams pleading for help.

To this day, students still play the mysterious board game in the campus dorms at Riverside College, and the legendary horror story of Ryan Banks lives on.

Sleep with the lights on,

Sydney

# OUIJA

*A board game used to contact the spirit world. Developed for commercial distribution in 1891. Named by Charles Kennard, founder of Kennard Novelty Company. While Mr. Kennard was playing the game, a spirit spelled out the word "Ouija". It is an ancient Egyptian word that means "good luck".*

# One

Rachel Thomas swept her long, tousled brown bangs out of her eyes. She steadied her hands on the steering column as she raced away from the haunted house where she had grown up. Plagued by the spirits of an unknown entity that had dwelled in her home for more than ten years, she had managed to accept her paranormal existence in a world where most people had never heard of such things. Or maybe they just didn't tell anybody about their experiences. Maybe there were many more people just like her who were afraid to talk about real life hauntings. But this was a time of new beginnings, the beginning of the rest of her life when the hopes and dreams of the past could become the realities of the future. If she could put the hauntings to rest, she could concentrate on what was before her. In just two weeks, she would be starting classes as a freshman at Riverside Community College.

Riverside was a small town college nestled near a centuries old river where Indigenous people once lived and played. Riverboats filled its waters, and the Spanish explorer, Hernando De Soto once crossed its shores. The river had a history that seemed to stretch as far as its 200 mile long waters, but it was a history of prosperity, tragedy, and death that still lived on in legendary ghost tales.

Rachel drove her silver 1983 Buick Regal into the front parking lot that faced her future home. Kendall Hall was one of eight dormitories for housing students. Although Rachel had been unable to secure her first choice of living arrangements in the college's most updated facilities, she was excited and anticipating the arrival of her new suite mate whom she had never met.

She turned the ignition off, pushed the door open with her foot, and got out of the car. She stretched her hands above her head and stood still for a moment as she surveyed the empty parking lot and vacant grounds surrounding her. She thought about the first day of classes and how congested the campus would become. Year after year, the college's Fall enrollment had grown. With more than 3,500 students attending college at Riverside, the odds of finding an empty space close to classrooms would be next to impossible.

Rachel sighed and quickly turned her thoughts back to the car crammed full of clothes and personal décor taken from her room back home. Moving in would take a couple of hours. She slammed the car door shut and turned to look at the building's second floor windows. She contemplated the number of trips it would take to haul several loads of her personal belongings up the stairs. And although the housing department had already guaranteed that the room would be ready to move in, she hesitated to unload anything before checking it out.

Rachel walked toward the glass front entrance and opened the door. The stone gray building smelled like pine sol as she entered an empty foyer with two closet-like doors to the left and an apartment to the right that served as a residence for the Dorm Parent who oversaw the needs and security of the dormitory's students.

Rachel slowly walked straight ahead to the stairwell entrance that led to the second floor. The air near the stairwell was stuffy and hot causing her to cough, and the smell of fresh paint stung her nose. The building was eerily silent, and it reminded her of the late nights at the nursing home when she had gone to her mother's workplace after the old people had gone to bed.

She stepped forward onto the bottom steps and began to climb the stairs. First the bottom steps and then a turn to climb the last stairwell to the top. She stopped at the last step and pulled another door open that led to the second floor hallway. The steel door was heavy and creaked loudly as she opened it. The bottom of the doorplate slid across the floor, creating a long and creepy noise that echoed down an empty hall.

For a minute, Rachel felt an unease that she had often known before, but for reasons she couldn't explain. She glanced into the hallway before her and stepped forward letting her fingers slowly release the door as it closed shut, its spring mechanisms creating the sound of metal on metal.

Rachel stood still, her body rigid but fully aware of her surroundings. Her bare arms were covered in goosebumps as she tried to rub them away, but just then a loud bang echoed from the right end of the hall. She jerked around and faced the source of the noise only to observe an empty space. Her eyes were wide as she stared down the dimly lit hall now filled with an eeriness that she couldn't dismiss. It never failed. If there was an otherworldly spirit present wherever she went, it always seemed to find her.

Her breath seemed to hang in her throat, and she had to remind herself to breathe. She took a long, deep breath and closed her eyes for a moment. She then turned back around, brushed off her fears as best as she could and walked straight toward the left end of the hall where her dorm room was located.

She stopped in front of the door and reached for the silver doorknob. She twisted it to the left and pushed the door open, eager to get inside and settle in. The room was painted a blinding white with white mini-blinds, two dull, steel gray bunk beds, and a white tile floor. Inside the double closet was a small chest of drawers also painted white. And against the inside wall and facing the hallway was a built-in desk with shelves. Painted white.

Rachel let out a sigh. The place felt like a hospital room or worse a morgue minus the cold air. She walked over to the window beside the two bunkbeds and noticed that it was locked tight. She fidgeted with the locks, snapping them back and forth. She then inspected the bathroom that she would be sharing with her suitemates and found that it included a half tub/shower combination and one toilet. *Four girls with one bathroom. That should be interesting.*

Rachel's eyes roamed the room again as she considered what it would take to liven up the place. *Color, décor, girl stuff.* As she became swept away with the thought of college life and living in a dorm with her closest friends, she forgot about her unease just minutes before. And although her dorm room offered anything but a cozy feeling, she relished in the idea of college living.

She surveyed the room, deciding which bunkbed would be hers. Which side of the room would be hers for decorating? Closet space and desk space? She was silently considering it all when the abrupt sound of a door slamming shut brought her back to the present.

"Hello." The raspy and friendly voice of Josie Norton echoed in the empty room, bouncing off the white cinder block walls. She stood just inside the door that Rachel had left standing open.

Rachel whirled around and faced her new roommate who stared back at her with a bright, toothy smile and crystal blue eyes. Her messy, dark brown hair was hanging partially out of the ponytail she had fastened earlier that morning, and her extra-large AC/DC t-shirt hung loosely over a pair of faded blue gym shorts.

Rachel smiled with a slightly startled look and responded. "Hi, you must be Josie!" She offered a handshake.

Josie accepted Rachel's hand with a firm and gregarious grip after sitting her guitar case down on the floor.

"Are you getting settled in early too? I've got a car

full of stuff from home." Rachel asked with a light-hearted tone.

Josie let out a boisterous, nasal laugh and nodded. "Yeah, I've got a couple of trips to make to get it all here. Oh, this is the closet space, huh?" She pointed to the two closets, each containing a small chest and barely enough room to hang a week's worth of clothes and a couple of coats.

"Yes, that's it. I can take the one on the right if that's okay." Rachel did not hesitate to designate ownership of personal space since she had to get started unloading her car.

"Oh, yeah, that works for me. Are you a heavy sleeper? How do you like the room temperature? I sleep like a bear and love a cool room." Josie asked wanting to get to know her roommate's compatibility.

Rachel smiled. "We'll get along beautifully. I'm a light sleeper, but the cooler, the better for me." Rachel shoved her hands in her Calvin Klein size 5 pants pockets.

Josie gave Rachel a thumbs up. "Cool. I'm gonna go grab a few things."

Rachel nodded. "Okay, I guess I should get started too." She started for the door and stopped as Josie paused in the doorway.

"Hey-- You ever played Ouija?" Josie asked.

Her eyes had a mischievous twinkle, but Rachel didn't respond with a lighthearted demur. Instead, her face turned pale. She felt as if the blood had just drained out of her body as her legs became weak. A strange silence lingered as she stared into the eyes of Josie Norton. Pale blue eyes that now seemed to flicker with a curiosity destined for danger. Then without warning, the same dreadful unease that slapped Rachel Thomas in the face as she entered the upstairs hall returned. And a premonition materialized before her, seizing her in a vision of horror.

# *Two*

The door slammed shut behind Josie, leaving Rachel in a cold reality of what was to come. She took a breath and reached for the doorknob as she whispered to herself and vowed to warn her new friend of the board's dangers. *But most people don't listen.* She skipped down the stairs and out the front door.

Josie disregarded Rachel's silence as nothing unusual and walked past her carrying a large box with clothes draped over the top. Rachel grabbed an armful of belongings out of her car and followed her back inside the building and up the steps.

"Hey, Josie, do you believe in haunted houses?" Rachel began a series of interrogating questions.

"I don't know. Maybe." Josie paused and then asked. "You're scared of the Ouija board, aren't you?"

Rachel dropped the armful of clothes onto the bunk bed resting against the inside wall of the room. She picked up a couple of hangers that dropped to the floor.

"Ouija boards are evil. You haven't heard about the terrible things that can happen after playing with one?"

Josie's eyes grew big. She placed the box on the floor near her closet and began to hang clothes on the steel closet rack. "Like what?"

"Like demon possession and evil things. Like being haunted by something that comes out of the board." Rachel felt a chill.

Josie laughed. "No, I don't think that's true. It's just a game. That stuff is not real. But wouldn't it be cool if it really could talk? We could ask it all kinds of stuff."

Rachel shrugged and pretended not to care. "Well, I can tell you from firsthand experience that I've lived in haunted houses, and it's no fun. It can be scary as hell."

Josie turned her attention to the box and flipped the

top flaps open as she considered how to respond to Rachel's fears. She then slid the hangers to the end of the closet.

The loud sound of old, creaking wood and sliding drawers filled the room as Josie examined the empty chest pushed against the inside closet wall. There was hardly enough space to hold her personal items, and she quickly realized that she would have to send most of her belongings back home.

"Do you have your schedule yet?" Rachel decided to change the subject.

"Yeah, I think so. Oh, and don't worry. We don't have to play that game here. A couple of my friends use to play it, and they said that they heard The Center of Performing Arts here on campus was haunted."

Rachel stopped hanging up clothes and smiled at Josie. "So you *do* believe in ghosts?"

Josie smiled back. "Well…"

Rachel continued. "And you have played with a Ouija board before?"

Josie nodded, then asked. "Have you?"

"Only once. But my sister has many times, and that's

the reason my room was haunted. She wouldn't stop until it scared her, but now we've got a ghost that we can't get rid of. It hurt her one time."

"What do you mean?" Josie was getting creeped out but couldn't contain her curiosity.

"It used to cause things to fly across the room. Like books and trinkets that she had sitting on a cupboard. One night it woke us up after midnight. We heard a loud crash, and when my sister got up to turn on the light, a porcelain plate hit her in the face and cut her cheek."

Josie's mouth fell open and she exclaimed. "No shit! That's crazy!"

"No shit." Rachel repeated. "It happened. And my sister had been playing with the board earlier that night."

"And you saw it?" Josie asked.

"Yeah, my sister and I used to share a bedroom."

Josie placed a row of t-shirts in the second drawer. "I was always told that my great grandmother used to work magic, and she believed in evil spirits. She—

Rachel waited to hear more, but Josie broke off into a disturbing silence as she stared past Rachel's shoulder. Rachel spun around to see a flicker of light zipping past her and into the adjoining bathroom. Josie screamed and dropped the shirts in the floor as she raced out the door. Her scream echoed down the upstairs hall while Rachel stood paralyzed. She breathed slow and finally walked backwards out the door.

As soon as reached the hall, she turned and bolted down the stairs and outside the building where she met Josie now laughing as if she had just pulled off a prank. They rested against Rachel's car and Rachel stared at Josie in disbelief.

"What the hell was that?" Rachel asked, wiping her hand across her forehead.

Josie shook her head. "Let's not panic. Maybe it was just a sunbeam coming through the blinds. We've got ourselves too worked up talking about this stuff."

Rachel finally busted into laughter. "You should have seen yourself! You threw those clothes half-way across the room and ran like hell!"

Rachel then began to point her finger in the air and move it back and forth as she declared. "I'm not going to let a ghost scare me out of my dorm. It was nothing."

Josie let out a short laugh and nodded in agreement.

She leaned back against the car, stretching her arms above her head and then pushed her body away as she started for the door. As the girls climbed the stairs, Josie began telling Rachel about her singing and guitar playing.

"I'll have to play for you sometime. I've been playing since I was a kid." Josie bragged. It was the one thing that had satisfied a loneliness she struggled to overcome as a foster child. She didn't remember many days of living with her biological mother, but she remembered every single day that she had lived without her.

The two young women climbed the stairs and re-entered the hall. They continued the short walk back to the last door on the left, Room 205, but just as they turned to enter the room, they heard a distinct shuffling sound and froze dead still in the doorway.

Josie lightly touched the middle of the door and pushed it open. The bottom of the heavy, metal door scraped the floor as it opened. And then Rachel let out a terrifying scream that shook them to the core as Josie gasped at the eerie sight just inside the room.

Stacked neatly on the floor in front of them was Rachel's unsorted clothes, but lying face up on top of the pile was Josie's Ouija board with the planchette positioned over the word *Yes*.

# *Three*

FOUR WEEKS LATER.

Rachel struggled to open her eyes. She sensed that someone was in the room with her, but she couldn't get awake. It was as if something was forcing her into a strange comatose state where her hearing and senses were alert, but her reflexes were paralyzed. And her thoughts dangled between a waking awareness and a descent into lucidity.

For the past fourteen days, she had remembered the disturbing Ouija board incident. Although the board had most likely been laying there on top of the clothes the entire time and unnoticed by the two girls, neither one of them denied the fact that it had unnerved the hell out of them. Josie had agreed to remove the board from their room by giving it to a friend for safe keeping, but the lure of its mystery continued to taunt them day and night.

No one else was there in the dorm room except Rachel. She was alone for the third straight night that week. College life had quickly settled in on her and her new roommate. She spent long days in classrooms and after school cheerleading practices, but Josie rarely came back to the dorm room before the early morning hours. By then, Rachel was usually getting awake for the start of another day of back-to-back classes.

The two girls shared little in common except for their love of the performing arts and a mutual past childhood in a dysfunctional environment. Josie was embracing her newfound freedom by staying out all night, skipping classes, and making new friends. She was the type of person who accepted everybody. Regardless of their religious convictions or lack of religion, Josie welcomed them into her circle. And it was a circle that was growing fast with atheists, Buddhists, backsliding Baptists, and Wiccans who only practiced Paganism because it was considered cool.

Rachel began to stir, slowly moving her feet against the cool soft sheets. The room's temperature was a chilly 68 degrees as the wall air conditioner still hummed after hours of running full blast. She pulled her favorite two quilts closer to her chin. Outside, the sun had just begun to peak through the tiny slits in the window blinds.

Rachel rolled onto her right side facing the wall as the A/C unit shut off making the room too quiet for her liking. She listened to the stillness and thought about her ex-boyfriend who had conveniently ended their eight month relationship when his prospects began to increase. He had been her first real boyfriend and even though she thought he was a cheap bastard at times, she loved being with him. She remembered the smell of Ralph Lauren Polo cologne that he always doused himself with moments before their weekly date. Her eyes remained closed as she imagined the smell, almost bringing it to life until a sudden tap on the ceiling terminated her tranquility.

Tap. Tap. Tap.

Rachel's eyes flew open. She scanned the room from side to side but wasn't able to see anything. It was still thirty minutes before sunrise. Her mind raced. *Why hadn't the alarm clock gone off yet?* She had a routine that she followed to a tee, always getting up at 5:30 a.m. to shower and dress before heading to the cafeteria for breakfast.

Rachel sensed an invisible energy in the room. She imagined that it was hovering above her bed and floating around the room. Her heart started to pound, and she felt as if she was about to lose her breath. She was almost too scared to move, but she fought against her fear and in one fast, vehement movement she jumped from the bed and flicked the light switch on.

The fluorescent lights swept away the dark and illuminated the small room. Rachel took a deep breath and shook her head with aggravation and a sense of relief. She had known these feelings many times before, but there was no getting used to paranormal activity, no matter how benign it might be.

Rachel grabbed her robe and headed for the shower,

but just as she stepped foot into the closet sized bathroom, Josie bolted through the door.

"Good morning, sunshine!" Josie's slurred greeting was followed by incessant giggles.

"Good morning, Josie. Are you going to make it to Biology today?" Rachel imitated Josie's slurred speech.

Josie grinned. "Uh, probably not, but oh shit, I need to."

Rachel laughed. "I'm gonna get a shower and head to breakfast. You wanna join me?"

"Oh, no. I'm beat. Don't worry. I'll be at Biology. I'm just gonna catch a couple hours of sleep." Josie yawned and laid down without bothering to remove her clothes or change into sleepwear. Her sneakers fell to the floor at the end of the bed as she pushed them off one foot at a time.

"Ok. Hey, before you go to sleep—You moved that Ouija board out of here, didn't you?"

Josie rolled over and looked at Rachel. "Yeah, I gave it to Stephanie. She's got it in her room."

Rachel gave Josie a thumbs up.

Josie rolled her eyes with a silly grin. "But hey

listen—Tomorrow night, there's a group of us that are going to meet in front of Eastside Hall. You should come. I want you to meet Spencer. He's so cool!"

Rachel smiled.

Josie rolled back over facing the wall and closed her eyes. She then called out just as Rachel turned the shower faucet on. "And tomorrow night is Ouija."

The water drowned out Josie's last words as the shower stream trickled down Rachel's back. In less than twenty-four hours, a hellacious battle would begin. A battle deep in the subconscious realms of a human's most vulnerable state. Nightfall would become the most dreaded part of the day when sleep became imminent and malevolent spirits of non-human entities came alive.

# *Four*

Rachel's eyes were heavy as she fought to get awake. Her eyelids were sealed tight as if they had been hammered shut.   She grunted and fought against an invisible force that seemed to slip back and forth between the dark recesses of her dreams and daylight.  Although Josie had moved the board out of their room, Rachel had mysteriously begun to dream about it.   Even in its absence, the board had left a haunting impression that she could not escape.

Strands of hair covered her face as she snapped her head from side to side against the pillow.  Once again, she sensed a presence in the room. *Open your eyes*. She felt her body falling back into sleep, and then she jerked awake. She squeezed her eyes shut and then without warning, she felt the hot moist breath of someone or something breathing in her face.

Her eyes flew open and she bolted upright, screaming like a wild animal. She breathed fast and hard as her eyes darted around the room, searching for something that had now disappeared.

Josie sat up, startled and confused. She kicked the bedsheet off in a mad fury. "What's wrong?!" She shouted.

Rachel wiped her eyes. She was shaking. "I don't know. Was I dreaming? Something was near my face! I felt its breath, Josie!" She was hysterical, sobbing uncontrollably.

Josie leaned forward and hugged her tight. "It's okay. You're awake now. But damn, Girl. You scared the hell out of me."

Rachel wiped her cheeks with her shirt sleeve. "It scared me worse."

"You're okay now? It was just a bad dream, right?"

Josie's efforts to calm Rachel helped.

Rachel nodded once and closed her eyes. "Yeah, I think so."

Josie lay back in the bed and raised her left arm in the air as she examined the watch on her wrist.

"Damn, it's time to get up." She ran her fingers through her hair and stared at the ceiling.

Rachel slowly positioned her feet on the floor and stood up. She reached for the clothes that she had laid across a nearby chair the night before and began to pull her jeans on. Her mind was consumed with thoughts of the invisible breath she had just encountered. *It felt so real.*

She then finished getting dressed, brushed her hair, and grabbed her backpack as she headed out the door to breakfast. She called back to Josie before shutting the door.

"See you later, Josie."

Josie rolled over to her left and threw her legs over the side of the bunk bed.

"Okay, Girl, see you later. Don't forget about tonight! Eastside Hall, 8:00 p.m."

The door clicked shut. Rachel turned and stared down an empty, dimly lit hall. The soft glow of bedside lamps escaped from underneath a few doorways. Rachel stood motionless as the same familiar feeling of being watched returned. That same scary, anxious feeling of butterflies in the stomach overwhelmed her, and she sprinted toward the hall exit door. She busted it open and raced down the stairs.

## *Later that evening. 8:20 p.m. Eastside Hall*

Dusk had already settled and nightfall was closing in as Rachel drove around the deep curve leading to Eastside Hall. Her mouth fell open in surprise as she neared the front of the building where dozens of students had gathered to hang out in the front courtyard. Lawn chairs were placed in a large circle that enclosed the group and several outdoor lamp posts illuminated the area.

Rachel pulled into the nearest empty parking space and turned the engine off. She watched the conviviality of the students for a moment before joining them. As she reached for the car door handle, she caught a glimpse of Josie running around the circle as she was being chased by a tall, dark-haired guy wearing a faded Iron Maiden 1984-85 World Slavery Tour t-shirt and ripped jeans.

Rachel smiled to herself. *That Josie is a wild thing.* Rachel then released the latch and pushed the door open but just as she stepped out of the car, Josie noticed her and came bouncing over.

"Hey, you made it! Get over here, Girl! You've got to meet Spencer." Josie's energy was infectious. Wherever there was a group gathered, she would quickly become a star.

"Is Spencer the same dude that I just saw chasing you around the circle?" Rachel laughed.

"Oh, you saw him? Yeah, that's him." Josie grinned.

Rachel slammed the door shut and followed Josie to the courtyard. She was pleasantly surprised by the number of attractive guys who had shown up. She was expecting to see a group of metal maniacs and band junkies smoking cigarettes and comparing tattoos, but there was a diversity of personalities among the fellowship circle. And many of them were people she recognized from The Performing Arts Center. People whom Josie already knew from her involvement in the college's music programs.

Spencer gave Josie a toothy grin as she and Rachel approached. "Hey, Spence. I want you to meet my roommate, Rachel."

Spencer nodded and flung his arms out as if he were inviting Rachel for a hug then quickly put one arm down and offered a handshake instead. "How's it going, Rachel? I've heard all about you."

Rachel shook Spencer's warm, calloused hand. "Has she? Oh, you better not believe any of it!" Rachel joked.

Josie huffed. "I told him how pretty you are. Gorgeous hair. Gorgeous eyes. Beach body. Little Miss Perfect." Using both hands, Josie traced an hourglass shape in mid-air and motioned toward Rachel, indicating her roommate's slender figure.

Rachel shook her head. "Oh, no. Definitely not me."

Josie rolled her eyes and changed the subject. "I'm so glad you came. You remember Stephanie?" Josie grabbed Rachel by the arm and pulled her away. Spencer chuckled and winked as he held up two fingers, offering a peace sign.

Josie and Rachel took three steps forward and then Josie abruptly stopped. She threw her hands in the air. "Wait. There's my song!"

Spencer mimicked her response to the opening sound of Whitesnake's *Still of the Night* playing on the local radio channel. He bent down and maxed out the volume on the Sony Boom Box that was situated on the ground and facing the inside of the circle. The profound and explosive sound of drums and electric guitars burst forth causing everyone to pause and turn toward him.

Two guys standing near Spencer joined Josie in the center of the circle as they simulated the band's lead singer playing the guitar. The circle of friends was now rockin' and rollin' to a Top 40 hit.

Rachel pointed and laughed at Spencer's audacious impersonation of David Coverdale, the lead singer of Whitesnake. She shook her head and turned away, then stopped dead still as her body became chilled at the sight of Stephanie Baker removing a Ouija board from its box.

Josie immediately noticed Rachel's rigid stance. She hurried to Rachel's side, leading her by the arm toward Stephanie Baker, almost dragging her across the lawn.

"Hey, Steph. This is my roommate. It's about time you two meet!" Stephanie's eyes moved down Rachel's body in a once over as she offered a half-cocked smile. Her green eyes seemed to glow against her pale skin and dyed black hair.

"Hey." Rachel took note of Stephanie's cool demeanor. Although her tone was friendly, her greeting was brief and reserved.

"Hey. It's nice to meet you." Rachel smiled and offered Stephanie a handshake as the only mannerly thing she could think to do. She felt somewhat awkward and creeped out as Stephanie held the Ouija board next to her chest as if she was guarding it.

Stephanie reached out and accepted Rachel's handshake. Then she looked at Rachel as if she had just recognized a long lost friend. She pointed at her and spoke with an inquisitive tone.

"Oh yeah, I just remembered. Josie told me about you. She said you were scared of the Ouija board."

Rachel laughed, pretending to ignore the remark, but in a way, it pissed her off.

"Nah, I'm not scared of it. It's just creepy. I've heard some bad stuff about it."

"Like what?" Stephanie wasn't giving up.

Rachel took a deep breath. "Well, I've heard that you never really know who the spirit is that you're talking to."

"So you've tried it before?" Stephanie's curiosity grew. Her eyes were wide as she waited for Rachel's response.

Rachel was beginning to feel uneasy. She shook her head and frowned.

"Not really. Maybe once, but nothing much happened." She lied.

Stephanie nodded.

"Me either, but I've always wanted to see if it really works. This is Amber Simmons, by the way. She says the board is real." Stephanie motioned to a short, red haired girl with a pale, freckled face and skinny legs standing next to her. Amber took a drag off her cigarette and exhaled, blowing smoke upward as she tilted her head back.

"Yeah, I've used the board before. But it can scare the hell out of you." Amber reaffirmed Stephanie's comments.

Rachel's skin grew cold. Just then several other students began to gather around as Stephanie and Amber sat down in the soft, green grass. The two of them positioned themselves close together, their knees touching as they sat Indian style. Stephanie then rested the board between them and placed the planchette in the center.

Rachel was edgy as Stephanie placed her fingertips onto the planchette. The music and voices coming from the group began to fade into the background, and the only thing she heard was the sound of Stephanie's voice as she began to move the board's communicator around in circles.

First to the alphabet. Next to the numbers at the bottom of the board. And then she paused in the center and began to summon the spirits. Amber rested her fingertips next to Stephanie's as she stared into her eyes.

"Is anybody here? We want to talk to you."

Nothing changed.

"We know you are here. Tell us your name."

The planchette moved. "Amber, stop moving it. That was you." Stephanie said with aggravation.

"Sorry. I always get a little nervous at first." Amber apologized and leaned back, removing her hands and wiping her sweaty palms across her jeans. She then placed her fingertips back on the board.

"We want to talk to you. Are you here?" Stephanie asked again and began to move the planchette across the board as if the movement might spawn some action.

"My name is Stephanie, and this is Amber. We want to know our future. Can you tell us?"

The board was silent.

Stephanie's tone became more demanding and agitated as she pressed for the spirits to speak.

"Why are you hiding? Don't you want to talk to us?" Stephanie stopped moving the planchette.

Then without warning, the planchette slid across the board in one violent sudden motion. Everyone gasped and jumped back. Amber grabbed the board as Stephanie jerked. And fear washed over Rachel like a tidal wave as she looked down at the planchette with its center resting clearly on the word "YES".

Rachel backed away, one foot at a time. The creepiness overwhelmed her, and she couldn't make herself stay. No matter what any of them said about her, she couldn't watch what was happening because she knew that Amber Simmons and Stephanie Baker wouldn't stop until they were satisfied that the spirit was real. An awareness took over Rachel Thomas at that moment. The premonition that she had seen played before her weeks ago was now staring her in the face.

As Rachel neared the sidewalk, she watched Amber and Stephanie put their hands back on the planchette and summon the spirits again. Then Rachel turned and ran. She ran as hard as her legs could carry her back to the car. She jumped in and sped away toward the dorm, leaving Josie behind.

As she parked the car and entered the building, she distinctly heard someone call her name, but no one was there. No one that she could see. And she knew. Without any doubt, she knew that something had been awakened. And it was coming. In the most hostile and vile way imaginable, the spirit was about to be unleashed.

# *Five*

## *Hours later...*

The dorm room was almost pitch black except for the soft glow of a nightlight that Rachel had placed near the bathroom entrance. Josie drifted in and out of sleep until the faint sound of a whimper disturbed her slumber. Then the sound of metal scraping against metal caused her to shudder. The sound continued, increasing with intensity each second. Josie grunted and rolled to her left side. She slowly opened her eyes and glanced around the room. Suddenly she saw movement. Her eyes froze as she stared inside her closet across the room where a group of clothes hangers now swung back and forth. Her body became paralyzed with fear, and she quickly looked away and fixed her eyes on Rachel lying in the bunk bed below her. Something was in the room with them, but she couldn't find her voice to scream.

Rachel was tightly nestled underneath a bed of quilts and at least one blanket. Her breathing was heavy, and her eyelids fluttered with a random strangeness that she had never seen. She studied Rachel with a perplexed expression and then jerked back as Rachel began to whimper louder. She watched Rachel toss to the right and then left, slinging her arms in the air as if she was fighting an invisible aggression.

Josie's eyes filled with tears. She struggled to overcome her fear as she watched Rachel fighting against an invisible aggression, but she realized that she had to get out of the bed. Somehow, she had to make her limbs move. She closed her eyes and gritted her teeth. Then in one swift motion, she jerked upright and quickly crawled to the end of the bunkbed. She climbed onto the ladder, moving down two steps at a time.

Rachel was battling something fierce in her sleep, and her thrashing about was now causing the bed to slide forward on the polished tile floor. The sound of metal scrapping against the tiles pierced Josie's ears.

"Shit!" Josie covered her ears and stumbled as her feet hit the floor. She reached out to shake Rachel awake, but just as her hands touched Rachel's arms, Rachel jerked upright and delivered a blood curdling scream that sent Josie falling backwards.

"Rachel! Wake up! Wake up!" Josie screamed, her body now trembling all over. She reached out and took Rachel's hand that was now stretched out in front of her and squeezed it hard.

"What the hell? It's okay—No, wait. Oh God. Help. Let me get the light." Josie stuttered in a panic stricken tone, her words a rambling mess. She rushed over to the light switch and flicked it on, then rushed back and sat down on the end of Rachel's bed.

"What the hell was that all about?" Josie asked, staring in horror at Rachel's pale, sweaty face now covered in strands of loose hair that was glued to her cheeks.

Rachel's body shook as she wiped tears away from her eyes. "I had another terrible dream. Oh God, it was scary. I'm so glad I'm awake but—

Rachel abruptly stopped talking and covered her mouth as she stared at Josie. She looked around the room.

"It's real, Josie."

"Damn, Girl. This is the second dream you've had, and I think I heard something. Or saw something. Hell, I don't know." Josie was afraid. She had little experience with supernatural phenomena, but she was finding it hard to deny its existence.

Rachel nodded. "Damn is right. It was horrible. I was dreaming about Amber and that damn Ouija board."

Rachel sobbed. "I saw something, Josie. Something bad. It was after Amber. Stephanie and Amber shouldn't have taunted that spirit last night."

"This shit creeps me out. I'm scared to tell you, but—

"But what?" Rachel turned her head sideways and looked at Josie with curious eyes.

"Something woke me up. I heard a noise coming

from the closet, and when I opened my eyes, I saw the hangers swinging back and forth."

Rachel's mouth fell open and a look of terror washed over her face. "It was in the room with us. Oh my god. It wasn't a dream."

Josie shook her head and leaned forward, but her entire body cringed with fear. And even though she knew that she had not imagined the swinging hangers, she tried to convince herself that it wasn't real. What she didn't understand, she didn't want to believe. And although her roommate's dramatic nightmare had just utterly unnerved her, she didn't want to feed Rachel's fears by admitting her own. Instead, she chose to deny it.

"It's not real, Rachel. It's just a game."

"I don't know." Rachel shrugged her shoulders and slowly began to relax.

A sudden knock at the door startled the two girls, causing them to jump forward, grabbing onto each other. Then a familiar voice came from the hall.

"Ladies, open the door. This is Ms. Ruth, the dorm mother."

Josie jumped up, unlocked the door, and opened it to

see Ms. Ruth dressed in a pale, pink house robe with coffee stains down the front. She peeked around the door and peered inside the room.

"What are you girls doing? It's almost three o'clock in the morning."

Josie stood in the doorway, not offering for Ms. Ruth to come inside. "We're not doing anything."

"Something is going on. The noise woke me. Are you moving furniture at this time of night?" Ms. Ruth asked in an aggravated tone. Her stringy, oily gray hair was planted firmly against her head, and her tightly pursed lips indicated that she was pissed.

Both Josie and Rachel shook their heads, then Rachel offered an explanation. "I was having a terrible dream, Ms. Ruth. I apologize. I think the bed slid across the floor a little. Maybe that's what you heard."

Ms. Ruth looked at Rachel and Josie through furrowed brows and suspicious eyes. She rested her hands on her hips and then ordered them back to bed.

"Ok, then. Just remember, your room is directly over my apartment. You girls get some sleep now."

"Yes, Ma'am." Josie agreed and slowly closed the

door. She looked back at Rachel.

"That sucks. I hate that we got stuck in a room right over her apartment." Rachel said.

"No shit. And she looks scary as hell." Josie agreed with a nervous laugh.

Rachel sighed, and looked up as the bathroom door opened and one of their suite mates walked into the room.

"Hey, what's going on? We heard somebody scream." Michelle Smith, a freckle faced gymnast who shared the adjoining room with two other girls peered around the door, her eyes wide with fright.

Rachel motioned for her to come in. "It's over now. Looks like I woke up the whole dorm." She said apologetically.

"Are you okay?" Michelle walked over and stood in front of Rachel now sitting up on the side of the bed.

"Yeah, just a bad dream." Rachel attempted to downplay the severity of the nightmare, but nobody was buying it. Her screams had been disturbing. The kind that reaches down to the soul and leaves an imprint of the terror she was experiencing.

"We heard Ms. Ruth at your door." Michelle continued to probe.

Josie nodded. "Yeah, she heard it too. Everything's cool now though. We better get back to bed." Josie didn't want to discuss it any further. She had just witnessed a paranormal event and her roommate caught up in a nightmare that shook her to the core. The scene of Rachel thrashing about bothered her immensely, and she wanted to forget about it.

Michelle turned to walk out. "Okay, goodnight. Glad everybody is okay over here."

"Thank you." Rachel called back to Michelle as she laid back against the pillow. She pulled the covers over her legs, and then leaned over to the bedside table. She pulled open the front table drawer and slid her fingers across the inside, searching for the small Native American dreamcatcher that her sister had given her for Christmas the year before.

"What are you looking for?" Josie walked over to the bed.

Rachel pulled the small dreamcatcher out of the drawer and hung it on the bedpost. "This. It's a dreamcatcher. The Indians believed that it would catch bad dreams before they could reach you."

Josie was amused. "Oh, cool. I love the feathers. And it's even got a couple of little bells."

Rachel rolled her eyes. "Whatever. I'd hang a damn eagle's nest on the wall if I thought it would help."

Josie busted forth with loud laughter. "We need to get a lamp in here. That nightlight of yours isn't enough. It's too dark." She flicked out the overhead light.

"Yeah, we do. Turn on the bathroom light and close Michelle's door so it won't bother them." Rachel suggested as she stared at the ceiling, her eyelids becoming like ten pound weights forcing her eyes shut.

As she gave in to sleep, she fought to block out the sound of the spirit's whispers. Whispers that she had heard right before her screams. And then pain. Sharp, stabbing pains sliced through her abdomen causing her to grimace. Sleep. She needed sleep.

"Good idea." Josie pulled the joining suite door closed, leaving the light on and the bathroom door slightly open. She then climbed the bunkbed ladder and flopped back down on the bed. She sighed heavily and closed her eyes until daylight.

# Six

Almost two weeks had passed since Rachel's disturbing nightmare. Josie was back to her usual partying until midnight leaving Rachel in the room by herself most of the time. What she didn't tell Rachel was that Stephanie and Amber had been using the board almost daily in Stephanie's room at the end of the hall. And Josie was always there, sometimes stepping in to allow Amber a cigarette break. They were all playing with the board and getting quite good at summoning the spirits that roamed the college campus. Spirits that had been summoned before, but they shouldn't have been.

They should have been left alone. Or maybe the spirits had gotten quite good at controlling them and invading their thoughts.

Josie sat across from Rachel and slouched down in her desk on the front row of Biology Lab. Biology I was their first class of the day and always the most dreaded since it started at 8:00 a.m. and required an alert mind ready to absorb every word the professor said. Most days Josie showed up for class unprepared and tired. She could barely keep her eyes open, but she made sure that she came to class often enough to prevent being kicked out for excessive absenteeism.

As Dr. Carolyn Foster lectured from the platform at the front of the room, walking from left to right, she looked down at Josie and noticed her staring in a wide eyed stance. Josie's face was fixed in a wicked grin that mimicked a circus clown as she stared at the professor. She forced her eyelids to widen and then squint, back and forth several times until all of a sudden, she pretended to be having a seizure and slumped down in her desk. She jerked and shook while continuing to make silly wide-eyed faces at the professor. After three or four seconds, she busted out laughing.

"Do you need to be excused from my class, Josie?" Dr. Foster warned. She wasn't amused.

Josie quickly sat up straight in her desk and shook her head. She waved her hand in the air and replied. "No, sorry."

The class gawked at Josie, most of them unamused by her strange clownish display and others bewildered. Rachel silently wondered what had come over Josie to cause such bizarre behavior. *Was she crazy?* Josie's grades were already suffering. Her focus on the social scene versus academics was causing her to flunk out. She had discovered a newfound freedom from the constraints of an unloving home environment where only her screw ups were noticed, but she wasn't able to transcend into reality outside of that place. Now she was on her own and forced to dwell in a world where screws up were noted with much the same significance that her childhood had known, and the attention bathed her fragility.

Dr. Foster turned her attention back to the projector that was placed on top of her desk in the center of the room. She pointed to the week's chapter notes that were projected onto the wall, but she was visibly disturbed by Josie's strange act and stumbled over her words for a moment before easing back into a lecture about the building blocks of proteins.

No one uttered a sound as she sped through the lesson's content, not pausing to give anyone an opportunity to ask questions. As she discussed each heading, she quickly replaced the clear plastic film on the projector's platform with a new sheet and continued until thirty-five minutes later, she reached the fourth and final installment.

"Ok, Class, we'll pick up here on Wednesday. There will be a quiz on sections one and two. Dismissed."

Dr. Foster flicked the light off on the projector and waited as the students filed out of the classroom with Josie Norton being one of the first to bail out. She didn't want to waste a second of time or give Dr. Foster an opportunity to make her stay after class.

Rachel quickly followed, breaking into a fast skip as she rushed to catch up with Josie.

"Hey, wait up!" Rachel slowed to a fast walk when

she reached Josie's side.

"What was that all about?"

Josie offered Rachel a sheepish look. "I don't know. I was just being a dick, I guess. Did you see her face?" She changed her tone in one swift notion and chuckled with demented satisfaction.

Rachel's mouth fell open, followed by an 'oh my god' tone.

"Yeah, I saw it. She thinks you're a damn idiot."

"She'll get over it." Josie shrugged it off. "Hey, what are you doing tonight about 7ish?"

"Probably nothing. Studying maybe. I don't know. Why?" Rachel had no definitive answer or plans.

"Well, you may not feel comfortable, but there's a big group of us meeting at the music building later."

"To hang out?"

"Yeah, and there's a new guy that says he is an expert with the board."

"Oh my god. You guys are still doing that?" Rachel's mood changed in an instant. She was mad and dumbfounded at the same time. How could Josie even think about participating in a game of Ouija after what they had experienced?

But Josie looked at Rachel as if she was stupid for asking the question.

"It's so cool. Stephanie and Amber have contacted a spirit named Ryan Banks. He says that he was a student here a few years ago."

Rachel's interest piqued in spite of her aggravation. "Really?"

"Yeah, he's told them all kinds of stuff. He even knows about Amber's ex-boyfriend and what he did to her."

Rachel stopped. "Wait." She reached for Josie's arm. "What do you mean?" Rachel searched Josie's eyes as if she was waiting for her to say it was 'all a joke'.

"The spirit knows things, Rachel. It's amazing. And he is so nice. We really like him."

"Are you kidding me? I just—

Rachel's voice drifted off without finishing her thought. A tingling sensation started at the sole of her feet and crawled to the base of her neck. She remembered the last horrific dream that she had fourteen days ago, and she felt her entire body respond to the memory. But she was curious just like the others. She didn't want to be. She wanted to run in the opposite direction, but she risked looking foolish if she gave in to her fears. She started an internal dialogue, an attempt to talk herself out of any beliefs she might have in the paranormal. Back and forth. Like a tug of war between intuition and logic, she juggled the two realities until she was mentally exhausted. The final question that she asked herself was still the same one she had played over and over. *Was the Ouija board safe?*

She had never really had a believable experience with the board even though she had played with it a time or two. When she was just a kid, the neighborhood bully had a board that many of them played when he was able to convince some of them to visit his house. But after playing the board, he began having nightmares until one day, he and his family up and moved in the middle of the night.

"Come on over. It'll be fun. And you've got nothing better to do." Josie urged, snapping Rachel back to the present.

"Girl, it's not going to get you. It's just a game. You can't give in to whatever this is."

"I can't believe how easily you're dismissing what happened. You saw something too. In our room. Remember?" Rachel was shocked by Josie's sudden denial.

Josie shrugged and popped her knuckles. "Yeah, I know. But look, let's just go. It'll be fun."

Rachel sighed. I'll think about it." She then turned and waved her hand in the air as she headed to her next class.

"You better be there! I mean it!" Josie called out as she walked in the opposite direction toward the Student Activity Center.

### *The Performing Arts Building, 7:30 p.m.*

Rachel pushed past the crowd that had already gathered in the foyer of the Music Hall. Nate Larson, a twenty-year old Johnny Depp look-a-like was seated in the middle and surrounded by several empty chairs that would be filled within minutes. His hands rested on top of a Ouija board situated in his lap as he waited for a volunteer to join him.

As an out-of-state student, Nate had come to Riverside College for their renowned Art Department. Some of the most highly respected artists had gotten their start at the small town college under the instruction and leadership of talented professors and artists from all over the world. Riverside was a stepping stone for him, but it was an important one that would lay the foundation he needed.

He flicked his shaggy, brown hair away from his eyes and glanced up at the crowd standing before him. Rachel's heightened sensitivity picked up on Nate's quiet, peaceful nature, and she wondered how he had gotten suckered into hosting the Ouija board game that evening.

As his eyes moved across the faces of onlookers, he literally froze when he looked into the eyes of Rachel Thomas. Nate's warm brown eyes locked with hers, and the hazel eyed skeptic found herself connecting with him during that split second exchange. Nate extended his hand, palm up and motioned for Rachel to join him in the empty chair directly in front of him. Rachel immediately reacted with a smile and a wave of her hand as a polite rejection.

"No? Awe, come on. Why not?" Nate coaxed.

"It doesn't work that well for me." Rachel coyly explained.

"So you've tried it?" Nate pressed. He wasn't about to end the conversation now that he had it started. All eyes were on Rachel.

She slowly nodded. "Yeah, but it's been a long time."

"Come on and join me. Everybody else is a chicken shit." Nate chuckled as he waited for Rachel to step forward.

Rachel hesitated and then gave in to Nate's invitation. Josie cheered from behind as Rachel stepped forward and sat down. She rested her knees against his, the board touching both of their laps. Nate placed the planchette in the center of the board and positioned his fingertips on it. Rachel joined him and waited for Nate to take the lead, but instead he sat still, his head down and his eyes fixed on the planchette.

Rachel began to push the plastic, supernatural messenger across the board, sliding it back and forth from left to right as she began to summon the spirits.

"Is anybody here who wants to talk to us?" Rachel could still feel her fingertips pushing against the planchette, and she knew that it wasn't moving on its own yet.

"We want to talk to you." Nate chimed in.

"Can you answer some questions for me?" Rachel decided that she would ask the spirits about her last relationship and whether or not her boyfriend was cheating. She already knew the answers to those questions, but she wanted to test the spirits. She continued to lightly guide the planchette around the board until suddenly she felt it leaving her fingertips and moving on its own. Rachel gasped but managed to remain still so that the connection wasn't lost.

"Are you here now?" Her eyes were wide as the planchette moved slowly to the upper left corner and stopped. Everyone in the room stared down as the word *YES* stared back at them through the clear, round window.

"What is your name?" The planchette moved around the board but did not spell out a word. Rachel quickly asked another question.

"Do you know my ex-boyfriend, Jim?"

*YES.*

"Was he cheating on me when we were together?"

No answer. The planchette continued to move in a figure eight pattern.

"Is Jim my future husband?"

*NO.*

Rachel was mesmerized and could hardly take her eyes off the center of the board, but she wanted to know more. She wanted to know if she would reconcile with Jim. After all, he had been in her thoughts for the past six months.

"Will Jim and I get back together?"

The planchette began to race back and forth with a wild and out of control pace. The spirit was now spelling out words that made no sense. Rachel pressed again.

"Tell me. Will Jim and I get back together?"

The planchette swooshed to the upper right corner.

*NO.*

Then for two seconds it rested until Rachel went too far. She glanced over at Nate who now appeared to be in a catatonic state. His hands were moving with the planchette, but his head was hanging down and his face was expressionless as his mouth hung open.

Rachel felt a sudden twinge of nausea and swallowed hard. She silently reasoned that Nate's bizarre appearance was simply because he was focused and concentrating on the game. Then she opened up a Pandora's box. She invited it in.

"Is there something you want to tell us? Don't be afraid. You can speak through us. What is your name?"

Just as she muttered the last syllable, the planchette began to race across the board with a hostile urgency that was out of control. It began to stop and start on random letters of the alphabet. Rachel struggled to make sense of what the spirit was communicating.

K-I-L.

"K-I-L? What is that? Do you mean kill?"

*NO.*

D-E-A.

"I don't understand. What is your name?"

D-E-A-D.

"Whoa, man!" Spencer exclaimed just as the spirit became more and more agitated.

"Slow down!" Rachel screamed at the spirit as she desperately tried to keep her fingers on the planchette, but it was moving too fast.

She felt a sudden gush of air slam across her face, and a choking sensation consumed her as she glanced across at Nate who was now completely slumped over as if he was asleep.

In the same split second, a loud crash echoed throughout the building and Josie screamed setting off a panic that enveloped forty other onlookers. The crowd became hysterical as they scrambled to escape. Terrorizing screams bounced off the walls as people fell over chairs and grabbed at each other. The lights shut down and the windows vibrated with a pulse so violent the seal around the glass cracked and threatened to explode.

Rachel coughed and jumped back from the board, her hand on her throat. She stumbled backwards and fell against the floor as she stared in horror at Nate's strange comatose stance.

Her heart was pounding as she pushed both hands against the floor and stood up. Her feet moved quickly as she backed away from the scene. She then whipped around and raced behind the last of the screaming witnesses who now exited through the double glass doors.

Just as she passed through to the outside, she glanced back and saw the Ouija board fall from Nate's hands and hit the floor with a thud. Nate's body remained slumped forward, his arms now dangling at his side. Even though the crowd's hysterical screams echoed throughout the hall, Nate's body seemed frozen and unable to move. In that moment, he was unresponsive with his eyelids peeled back in a wide open stare. Into oblivion.

# Seven

"Somebody's got to go back for Nate!" Rachel yelled. "Josie, wait. We can't leave him."

Several members of the crowd stopped in the courtyard that was located a short distance from the building. A group of girls huddled in a corner, visibly shaken as they discussed the consequences of summoning spirits through the board.

Josie halted and swung around. She looked past Rachel's shoulder and toward the glass window where she saw Nate now struggling to stand. He stumbled and swayed back and forth as if he was drunk or under the influence of drugs. She tapped Rachel on the arm and pointed in his direction.

"Look at him. You can see him from here. What the hell is wrong with him?" Josie asked as she stared at Nate in horror.

Rachel shifted her attention to the window several feet away as she witnessed Nate's dazed state. He seemed confused and off balance. "Oh my god. I don't know. Wait. He's coming out the door!" Rachel exclaimed.

Just as Rachel and Josie stepped forward to meet him at the door, Spencer noticed him and rushed over to help. He and Josie grabbed onto Nate's arms and led him to the courtyard as Rachel walked close behind. When they reached the grass, they slowly lowered him to the ground. He then leaned back and rested against his outstretched arms as he blinked his eyes open and shut several times.

"Hey, man. Are you okay?" Spencer patted his shoulder.

Nate took a deep breath then looked up into three sets of astonished and worried eyes as Rachel, Spencer, and

Josie waited anxiously for his response.

"I don't know what happened." He raised a hand in the air and motioned toward Rachel before he continued.

"I remember hearing Rachel ask some questions, and then everything just went dark. I fell into some sort of trance or something. What happened?"

The three of them looked at each other. Spencer spoke up, breaking the silence. "Nate, did you drink anything before you got here, man?"

Nate shook his head. "No, no. Nothing. What happened?" He pressed again, this time with agitation.

"You and I were playing the board. It just started to go crazy, and then all of a sudden, the lights went out and the windows and doors rattled so hard that we thought the whole thing was going to shatter. Everyone just ran out screaming minutes ago. Literally. It was just minutes ago. And you were just sitting there slumped over." Rachel knelt down at Nate's side.

"Damn. I feel sick. My whole body feels washed out." Nate's eyes were red and irritated. He rubbed his face and swept his dark, brown bangs away from his face.

"Yep, I'm done with that game. Let's get the hell out of here." Rachel said.

"Who's got the board?" Josie asked.

"Who gives a damn?" Nate looked at her in disbelief.

Rachel quickly chimed in. "Don't bring that thing to our room!"

"Oh hell no, of course not! But it belongs to Amber and Stephanie." Josie declared.

"Well, that's not our problem." Rachel stood up and started toward the nearby parking lot.

"Come on, guys. Let's go get something to eat. I'm not ready to go back to the dorm." Josie announced.

Spencer offered Nate a hand and assisted him as he stood. "Alright, who's driving?"

Rachel started for the parking lot as they followed her to the car. As she walked on ahead of Josie, she thought about her friend's involvement with Amber and Stephanie. *Just how much was she involved in the Ouija group that had now grown to nearly forty students on campus?*

Rachel reached the car and opened the door, allowing

everyone to get in. She cranked the engine and fastened her seatbelt. As she backed out and centered the vehicle in the street, she shifted the car in drive and then looked in the rearview mirror, locking eyes with Josie. She then issued a warning in the most solemn tone possible, her words blunt and clipped.

"Tonight was enough. This Ouija shit needs to end now before someone gets hurt."

Two hours later, Josie and Rachel dropped off Nate and Spencer at Eastside Hall. Rachel then drove across campus and parked in front of their dorm. Before Rachel could turn the ignition off, Josie jumped out and bolted for the front door.

"Hey, where you going?" Rachel called after her.

"I'll be right back. I'm just going to check on Stephanie." Josie replied.

Rachel frowned. She watched Josie enter the building as she got out of the car and slowly walked toward the door. Just as she reached for the door, she saw the back of Josie's heels climbing the stairs to the second floor. She paused and then hesitated to move forward. Something just didn't feel right. She couldn't shake that creepy feeling that something was waiting for her beyond her dorm room's door. She tried to brush it aside by telling herself that other than a bad dream and a creepy encounter with the Ouija board, there wasn't any reason for paranoia. And yet, it remained. Like a heavy fog penetrating rational thought, this premonition of doom continued to invade her mind, robbing her of any peace.

Rachel finally started for the stairs and stopped at the top step. She pushed open the door leading to the second floor hallway and peered up and down the corridor. The hall was dimly lit and vacant. Josie had vanished almost as soon as she had climbed the second staircase, but Rachel knew she had to take at least a few seconds to make it to the right end of the building where Stephanie's room was located.

Her eyebrows were scrunched together in a confusing look as she studied the end of the hall. She then spotted a trail of light, and she decided to sneak up to Stephanie's door. She figured if she got caught, she would play stupid and pretend that she was just about to knock and ask to join them.

Rachel tiptoed down the glossy, tile floor toward Stephanie's room. The other students were either sleeping or not home yet, but if she didn't hurry, she might get caught stalking her roommate, or that's what it would look like for sure. She held her breath as if she thought that would make a difference in the amount of noise her shoes made against the polished floor. She tiptoed in long strides from one end to the next.

Within seconds, she was standing at Stephanie's door. The absence of lighting near the right end of the building lent a darkness to the area making it difficult to see more than a few feet ahead. She moved in close to the outside wall, carefully placing her hands in front of her. Her heart pounded, and her stomach churned with butterflies as she leaned forward, her shoulders barely touching the door. She moved her head closer until her ear rested against the cold, metal surface. And then while quietly taking in soft and shallow breaths, she listened. She began to hear familiar voices inside the room, but their words were muffled. Then they began to speak louder, and their speech became clearer.

"Yes, but that spirit at the music hall wasn't the same spirit that me and Amber have been talking to?" Stephanie argued.

"How do you know? That shit scared everybody tonight." Josie argued.

"It wasn't the same one, Josie." Stephanie insisted.

Just then Rachel heard a creaking sound. She jerked back, expecting the door to open and then heard another voice inside the room.

"The spirit that we talk to committed suicide at Eastside Hall several years ago. Didn't we tell you?" Amber piped in.

"Yeah, yeah. Okay." Josie shrugged it off, pretending not to care.

Then shuffling sounds came through the wall as Rachel heard the soles of their feet sliding across the floor as they suddenly kneeled down and situated themselves in an Indian style sitting position. Stephanie took the board out and placed it on top of her legs.

"Are you staying?" Stephanie asked Josie.

Josie nodded and replied. "Sure, I'll stay just a minute. Open the window so I can smoke though, will ya?"

Stephanie looked up at Amber. "Hey, can you get the window?"

Amber walked over, unfastened the locks, and pushed the frame up exposing the night air. She peered out, checking to make sure nobody was standing below who could see smoke coming from their dorm window. Smoking was strongly prohibited.

"Hurry up, Josie. I don't wanna get fined for that shit if the old lady downstairs catches you."

Rachel heard Josie's footsteps moving toward the window as Amber sat down in front of her friend.

Stephanie began pushing the planchette, waiting for the ghost of Ryan Banks to come forward.

"Ryan, are you here?"

Rachel silently gasped. She suspected that they were still playing the board even after Josie had told them about the bad dreams she was having, but now she realized that her suspicions had been right. She was certain that they had been playing the board for weeks after removing it from her and Josie's room.

"Ryan, do you want to talk?" Amber asked again.

Rachel heard giggles and then a gasp.

"He's here." Stephanie confirmed.

"Ryan, did you know about what happened tonight at the music hall?" Amber continued.

Rachel could hardly breathe. Her mouth hung open and she became flushed. The humidity in the upstairs hall was always a problem, but the intensity of the moment seemed to magnify the hot damp air's effect.

Then a brief silence came from inside the room as Rachel maintained her position against the door.

"Ryan, were you there tonight?" Stephanie added.

Rachel wiped perspiration from her forehead. Although the metal door stood between her and the middle of the room, she distinctly heard the sound of the planchette's movement as it slid across the board and stopped on the word *YES*.

Amber stared at Stephanie. "He was there."

"Ryan, did you cause the windows to rattle tonight? That scared everybody really bad." Amber asked. The hair on her arms stood up.

Rachel heard the planchette slide across the board.

"No? Then do you know who did it?" Amber asked.

Several seconds passed without any sounds coming from the other side of the door. Finally, the sound of the planchette's plastic platform sliding across the gameboard indicated that the communication had not been broken.

"Can you spell their name?" Stephanie asked.

"Wait a minute." Josie broke the concentration.

"What? What is it? Damn, Josie, you ran him off." Amber said with irritation. The planchette abruptly stopped in the middle of the board.

"Let me get the hell out of here. I've had enough creepy shit for one night." Josie reached for the door.

Rachel suddenly jerked back and whirled around. She bolted for the fire exit door and hid in the stairwell as Josie walked out of the room. After the door slammed behind her, Rachel watched her friend's back as she walked toward their room. Then just as Josie disappeared from sight, Rachel hurried through the door and down the hall.

Once inside, Josie called out for Rachel.

"Hey, Rachel. Where are you?" She stopped in front of the sink and turned the hot water faucet on. She grabbed a washcloth hanging on the towel rack beside her and soaked it in warm water as she tossed a bar of face soap into the basin. She called out again.

"Hey, Rachel. You in the bathroom?" Josie continued her face washing routine as she lathered her face with suds and rubbed her cheeks in a circular motion. She closed her eyes for a moment as her fingers traced the soapsuds over her brows, and then she opened her eyes. Just then, she looked into the mirror and noticed Rachel's silhouette out of the corner of her eye as it exited the bathroom and walked behind her.

"Oh, there you are! Didn't you hear me calling you?" Josie placed the warm cloth over her face and wiped the suds off in a fast scrubbing motion. She quickly dipped the washcloth in and out of the basin of warm water and rinsed it out.

The silhouette of Rachel Thomas that she had just seen never responded, and an eerie feeling came over her as she glanced up and saw Rachel moving toward the door.  One step at a time, her feet marching to an unknown tempo.  Josie's face became locked in an expression of horror as fear paralyzed her.  She found herself unable to scream and then finally she managed to stutter instead.

"Rachel----what the---hell are you doing?"

She watched Rachel continue to move toward the hall joining the two suites until she disappeared from view. Then without warning, the door opened, and there standing on the other side was Rachel dressed in house slippers and carrying a ten ounce Dr. Pepper that she had gotten from a nearby vending machine.

Josie stared back at Rachel, her eyes wild and watery. Her face was chilled and still damp.  She coughed and sputtered, slinging the wet bath cloth over her mouth. She knew at that moment that her face must be deathly white from the horror of what she had just encountered. For the first time in her life, she had just seen a ghost. And the most terrifying reality of all is that it had masqueraded itself as Rachel Thomas.  Right before her eyes. *Or did it?*

# Eight

✝

"Oh my god, Josie. What's wrong? You're shaking." Rachel stepped past her and closed the door.

"Jesus. I just saw you. No lie. I just saw you walk past me while I was washing my face. You—You came out of the bathroom." Josie stuttered.

Rachel looked confused. "That's not possible. I wasn't even in the room."

"I swear to God." Tears spilled onto Josie's cheeks. Her legs trembled, and she turned and propped her hands against the sink.

Both of them felt a chill climb the length of their

bodies as they considered what Josie had just observed. They were afraid to close their eyes for the night, but sleep was a necessity, and it had a way of taking over. A way of forcing a body to surrender to unconsciousness. It was a vulnerability that neither Josie or Rachel wanted to risk, but there was no other alternative.

Finally Rachel spoke up. "Josie, I have a confession to make."

Josie stepped back and gave Rachel an inquisitive stare. "What is it?" Her pale, blue eyes continued to search Rachel's.

"Do you promise not to get mad at me?" Rachel implored.

"Maybe not. What the hell?" Josie waited.

Rachel shook her head as if to indicate that it was nothing and then confessed. "I know Amber and Stephanie are using the board. I heard them through the door."

Josie let out a sigh. "Is that it?"

"Well, yeah. I was afraid---

"I don't wanna be alone in here." Josie interrupted.

Rachel's entire body became rigid. "Me either."

"Until this whole thing dies down a little, let's just stay together. Okay?" If Josie had ever doubted the existence of a spiritual world, she was now transformed. Tonight, she was a believer.

"Let's try to get Ryan back, Steph." Amber coaxed her friend back to the sitting position in the middle of the floor. With Josie now gone, there shouldn't be any more interruptions in the room.

The two girls sat with their knees touching and balanced the board between them. They gently placed their fingertips onto the planchette.

"Ryan? Ryan? Are you here?" Stephanie called out.

"We want to talk to you. Please come back." Amber pleaded in an apologetic tone. "We didn't mean to scare you away."

The board slowly slid to the left and stopped. Amber looked up at Stephanie and whispered. "What's he doing?"

Stephanie shook her head. "I don't know."

"Ryan, do you want to talk?"

The planchette swooshed upward and stopped over the word *YES*.

Amber laughed. "Wow, Ryan. You came back in a flash that time." The planchette swirled around and landed back on *YES*.

"Can we ask you more questions about when you lived here?" Stephanie begged with a cautious tone.

*YES*.

She waited a few seconds and continued.

"How old were you when you died?" The pointer began to move to the row of numbers near the bottom half of the board.

*2*.

"You were 2 years old?" Stephanie asked, a confused smile covered her face.

*1*.

"No, he was 21." Amber answered without hesitation.

*YES*.

"How did you die?" Amber took over and continued

the line of questioning. The planchette hovered over the alphabet as it selected letters to form a word.

*G-U-N.*

"You were shot with a gun?"

*YES.*

"He's already told us this." Stephanie whispered.

"So? How else am I supposed to verify that it's really Ryan? Besides, he might tell us something different." Amber argued.

"Who shot you, Ryan?" Stephanie intervened, not wanting to lose her chance to ask the questions she wanted answered.

*M-E.*

"Do you mean that you committed suicide?"

*YES.*

"Why? Did something bad happen? Tell me." Stephanie asked a leading question hoping the spirit would provide more details about the days leading up to Ryan's suicide.

*S-A-D.*

"Oh, you mean you were depressed?"

*YES.*

"I'm sorry, Ryan. What made you depressed?"

The planchette began to pick up speed as it zipped back and forth in a figure eight.

"What the hell is wrong with him?" Amber was alarmed by the spirit's sudden mood change.

Stephanie shrugged. "I don't know. Ryan, I didn't mean to upset you. Calm down. It's okay." Their fingertips barely touched the edge of the planchette as it moved back and forth. It gradually slowed and settled in the middle of the board.

Stephanie breathed a sigh of relief. "Ryan, if it upsets you, we can talk about something else."

The spirit began to spell words again as it positioned the planchette above the alphabet in the center of the board and then zipped back and forth in short stops over each letter.

G-I-R-L.

"You had a girlfriend?" Stephanie said with a smile in her voice.

*YES.*

"That's sweet, Ryan. I'm sure she loved you very much." Stephanie suggested. She zeroed in on the board as if she could see the spirit of Ryan Banks through the planchette's window.

Amber looked at Stephanie. "Hey, I don't remember him telling us about a girlfriend."

Stephanie ignored Amber's remark. "Was she pretty?"

*YES.*

"What color hair did she have?"

Y-O-U.

Stephanie got a chill.

"She looked like Stephanie?" Amber asked with amazement.

*YES.*

H-U-R-T.

"You hurt her? Do you mean that you broke her heart?"

The planchette rested in the middle of the board, not moving.

"Ryan, did you hurt your girlfriend?" Amber persisted, but the planchette didn't move. Stephanie glanced up at Amber with wide eyes that silently screamed her fears at that moment.

"Is this Ryan?" Stephanie demanded.

The planchette didn't move, but the air in the room was thick as if something sinister had just moved in.

"Something's wrong. The tone has changed. It's not Ryan we're talking to. Say Goodbye quick!" Stephanie shouted.

In a split second and just as Stephanie and Amber pushed the planchette to the bottom of the board, it lifted up and sailed across the room, hitting the door and slamming to the floor. Amber jumped to her feet and raced to the door, flinging it open as she and Stephanie bolted out into the hall and down the fire escape stairwell. An hour would pass before they were brave enough to re-enter their room, but the ghost of Ryan Banks had never left. And no one had heard their screams at the other end of the hall. No, they were fast asleep and drifting into their own nocturnal nightmare.

# Nine

Nate and Spencer went their separate ways after Rachel dropped them off in front of the dorm. Nate kept his concerns to himself, but he inwardly struggled to overcome the sounds of panic filled screams and the haunting images that had settled deep within his psyche. He couldn't let go of the disturbing residual energy that had attached itself and penetrated his conscious after his experience with the board. It had been his first such encounter with the spirit world.

Raised in a church-going family, Nate came from a

long lineage of devout Christians. Although he was a silent practitioner of the faith most of the time, he didn't hesitate to express his personal beliefs in the presence of good and evil. And he knew that what he had witnessed in the music hall was not his idea of a good spirit.

Like so many other young adults who had played with the board during their days as a student on Riverside College campus, Nate Larson was in the wrong place at the wrong time. He was no different than any of the others who had ever played the game, but it was a game with terrifying consequences. And Nate was a willing participant with a naïve understanding of what he was engaging in.

Nate sat down on the edge of the bunkbed and leaned back. He was alone in a dorm room that he shared with no one. He had been a last minute enrollee who just happened to get a lucky break and be assigned the last corner room on the first floor of Eastside Hall.

He sighed heavily and stared at the ceiling. He blinked and fidgeted with the crucifix hanging from his neck as he tried to focus his thoughts on tomorrow's jam packed agenda. He had two days left to finish an abstract art project, and he didn't need any distractions that might hinder his progress. He rolled over to his left side and reached to turn off the bedside light. He pulled the lamp chain, and the room fell dark. Then he tested the alarm on his watch and laid it on the table as he settled back under the covers.

He closed his eyes and listened to the silence. The room was dead silent and calm except for the occasional humming that filled the air each time the A/C unit automatically shut on and off. Within seconds, Nate's waking state began to dissipate, his body drifting fast to sleep as his eyelids became too heavy to open. And he was utterly oblivious to the other presence now cohabitating in the room with him.

The bodiless spirit began to move the chair in front of Nate's desk. The legs on the metal chair scraped across the tile floor as it inched closer until it reached the side of the bed facing him. The lamp chain that dangled from the switch now began to dance and swing back and forth. A cold burst filled the room and swept across Nate's face causing him to stir. He grunted and pulled the blanket around his chin.

Then in an inexplicable surge, the bedside lamp flashed on and off, and Nate's watch alarm began to beep with a maddening speed that seemed to get louder with each flash. He jerked awake and turned to see the light flashing on and off. His eyes were wide with confusion as he reached to silence his watch alarm, but just as he started to swing his left leg over the side of the bed, he yelled.

"What the hell?!" He kicked the chair away from the bedside sending it sliding halfway across the floor. He leaped off the bed and flicked on the wall light, his body now terrified into a frozen stance as he stared into a room with no other tenants. His heart was pounding as he grabbed his sneakers and a t-shirt. He quickly pulled the shirt over his head and pushed his feet inside his shoes before grabbing-all in one swift motion-a pillow, his watch, and a blanket off the bed. He then bolted for the door and slung it open, not bothering to make sure if the door was locked as it closed behind him. He then ran to the opposite wing of the dorm, several doors down. He stopped in front of Room 101 and pounded on the door.

"Hey, it's me, Nate. Open the door, man."

Nate knocked again. This time harder. "Hey, man. Wake up. Let me in." Nate heard footsteps shuffling across the floor. Then the lock clicked, and the door opened.

"What the hell?" Spencer peered out at Nate through squinted eyes, his short black hair sticking straight up in a bedhead mohawk.

"I'll tell you in the morning, man. I just need to stay here right now." Nate pushed past him and entered the room as Spencer closed the door.

"Yeah, sure. Whatever, dude. But you ain't sleeping with me." Spencer crashed back on his bed.

"You ain't funny. I'm on the couch, Stud."

Nate plopped his pillow on the end of the couch and settled under the blanket. He sighed heavily and wiped his eyes. Then he massaged the pain that seemed to linger in his chest. The pain of an anxiety attack that felt like dozens of knives being driven deep into the center of this body. *What the hell had just happened? What the hell was in that room?*

Nate rubbed his forehead and began to whisper the 23rd Psalms.

*The Lord is my Shephard; I shall not want.*
*He maketh me to lie down in green pastures:*
*He leadeth me beside the still waters.*
*He restoreth my soul.*
*He leadeth me in the paths of righteousness for His name's*
*sake.  Yea, though I walk through the valley of the shadow of*
*death, I will fear no evil:  For thou art with me;*
*Thy rod and thy staff, they comfort me.*
*Thou prepares a table before me in the presence of mine*
*enemies; Thou anoints my head with oil;*
*My cup runneth over.*
*Surely goodness and mercy shall follow me all the days of my*
*life, And I will dwell in the house of the Lord forever.*

As the last words fell from Nate's lips, exhaustion overcame him, and his body surrendered to a deep slumber.

# Ten

## *Later the following Thursday...*

It was well past dusk, and the campus streets were quiet since most of the students had already settled in. The October nights were now becoming cooler and a welcome relief from hot humid days in the South. Rumors were circulating around campus about an upcoming vigil planned for the night before Halloween. In spite of the terror that dozens of students had experienced at the music hall, there were still the thrill-seekers who ignored danger and its consequences. And Amber Simmons had proudly announced that she had made friends with a Ouija spirit named Ryan Banks, passing her story around campus to anyone who would listen.

The overhead streetlights buzzed to life as Rachel, Josie, Stephanie, and Amber walked along the sidewalk to the Student Activity Building. It was the only building still open until 11:00 p.m. and often patrolled by the college's police department.

Rachel had invited Stephanie and Amber to hang out with the others. Josie knew what Rachel was up to, but she didn't question it. She knew Rachel was using the opportunity to confront them about what was going on with everybody. The freaky dreams and paranoia that nobody could ignore any longer. Rachel believed the chaos was being caused by negative spirits that had come through and attached themselves to her and Nate. And even though Josie claimed that she too was a victim of paranormal phenomena, she didn't trust Josie's promises to abandon the Ouija board circle. She was too close to Amber and Stephanie.

Amber peered through the front glass. Only the inside lights near the vending machines were still on in the front of the building. The back part of the building that housed the pool tables and an additional seating area was dimly lit with no remnant of student life left behind other than a few scattered chairs and a pencil or two that had been dropped onto the floor.

Spencer reached for the door and pulled it open. He allowed the others to pass in front of him before following Nate to the Coke machine while Amber arranged six chairs around a table. Stephanie dropped a couple of quarters in the machine.

"Hey, Amber. You want a Coke?" Stephanie punched a Grape soda selection, and it rolled to the bottom of the bin.

"Yeah, no wait! I want a Sprite." Amber turned and walked toward the small vending room as Stephanie dropped another fifty cents into the machine while Rachel debated over a Snicker candy bar and a Dr. Pepper.

Nate popped up around the corner of the door. "Hey, didn't you guys just eat dinner? Oink. Oink." He teased, trying to be funny, yet no one was laughing.

"This is dessert, Dude." Josie responded while everyone else ignored him.

The girls finished gathering their snacks and then followed Nate to the table where Spencer was already seated. He leaned back and forth in his chair, balancing it like a trapeze artist. Rachel frowned at him and studied his messy black hair and frumpy clothes. She wondered if he ever actually brushed his hair. She concluded that it looked more like a well-used broom with broken bristles sticking out in all directions, but his blue Superman eyes could melt kryptonite.

Spencer was a fun guy that everyone liked eventually. Even though some people thought his religious beliefs were weird, no one denied his ability to make friends. His atheism wasn't necessarily a result of his own choices, but it was rather a stance that he had taken. It was the only logical explanation that he could fathom for his childhood suffering. He accepted the absence of God in his life at an early age when God took his parents.

"You're going to bust your ass. You know that,

right?" Rachel took a seat next to Nate and warned Spencer, but he didn't seem concerned about the consequences.

Spencer laughed and let the front of the chair fall back to the floor. "Okay, guys. We all gathered here at Nate and Rachel's request. So spill it. What's going on?"

"And us too, Spencer. We're a part of this now." Amber spoke up.

"But you guys have been playing the game for weeks. Nobody even knew that you had that damn board until a couple of days ago." Rachel wasted no time and dove right in, confronting them head on.

"That's bullshit. Josie told you. You knew the board was in our room." Stephanie turned her eyes toward Josie with an accusing look.

"But you kept playing the game, Stephanie! Even after what happened to Nate, you two kept on!" Rachel yelled, her face turning red.

"Hey, hey. Everybody stop!" Nate interjected.

"Yeah, just shut up and calm down. Please. All of us are experiencing shit we can't explain since we opened up Pandora's box." Josie shouted. She stared down at the table and clasped her hands together, avoiding direct eye contact with Rachel or anyone else.

Spencer tapped on the table as if he were playing a set of drums. His apathetic demeanor was quickly agitating Rachel who gave him an evil look. She wasn't amused by his nonchalant attitude or his refusal to acknowledge what the rest of them had witnessed. She knew that Spencer was an atheist, but he was an irritating one at that moment.

Spencer glanced up and noticed Rachel staring at him as if she could go right through him. He put his hands in the air in an apologetic gesture and cleared his throat.

"You guys know I don't believe any of this shit. It's all in your damn head, but I'll listen."

Nate slammed his fist on the table. "It's not in my fucking head, Spencer. You don't believe in *anything* so keep your dumbass comments to yourself." Nate spewed back with venomous angst.

"Fuck you, Nate. I answered the door for you the other night, didn't I? I let you in." Spencer challenged.

"Yeah, you did. And I haven't slept in that room

since, but I can't keep sleeping on people's sofas, man." Nate shot back. He adjusted the front zipper on his jacket and tried to calm himself, but his anxiety was at a breaking point.

Everyone was quiet for a moment as Nate's comments sunk in. Nobody had an answer, but everybody agreed that they were experiencing a type of paranoia and ghostly phenomena that couldn't be explained.

"Look, we're all scared out of our ass now. Except for Spencer. I think we should all move into his place. He's the only one who can fight this thing." Josie joked.

The group broke into unrestrained laughter at Josie's quick attempt to lighten the mood, and it worked.

"Seriously, though, guys. I'm not comfortable being alone anymore." Rachel stated.

"Me either." Nate agreed.

Amber spoke up. "But the game started out fun. Steph and I were having a good time with it. And that guy Ryan—

"Amber, how do you know that this 'Ryan' was a real person?" Rachel interrupted.

Amber shook her head. She looked around the table. Everyone was now staring at her in anticipation of her response.

She shrugged her shoulders and then answered.

"I didn't. I never knew anything for certain. Just what he told me. He said that he committed suicide because he was depressed and had a bad experience here. He told us that he was 21 years old and had fallen in love, but the girl broke his heart. He also told us that he was a baseball player here."

Nate propped his elbow on the table and rested his chin in his hand as he listened. Rachel appeared to be making mental notes of everything Amber said.

"But that's not all he told us." Stephanie leaned forward.

"Yes, I know." Amber confessed.

"What do you mean?" Rachel and Nate asked at the same time, their voices in unison.

"He told us that he wanted to get revenge for the bad things that happened to him while he was a student here." Amber forced the confession. She had not bothered to tell Josie that the spirit had become hostile.

"Jesus." Nate whispered.

"We stopped playing with the board for a few days until a couple of nights ago. But I don't know who the spirit was that came through the other night." Amber's voice was nervous, but Rachel didn't trust it. She thought Amber was a fake.

"I'm going to find out who this 'Ryan' guy is. If there really was a dude named Ryan---wait, what was his last name?" Rachel asked.

"Banks. His name was Ryan Banks." Amber said.

"Ok, Ryan Banks. If this guy went to school here and committed suicide, there should be a record of it. I'm going to see if I can find out who he was." Rachel said with a stern determination.

Nate and Spencer nodded in agreement.

"I'll help you." Josie offered.

"Count us in too, but I don't even know where to begin looking for that kind of stuff." Stephanie resolved.

"I do. If Ryan Banks lived and died here, there should be a newspaper story or a picture of him in one of the yearbooks."

"You're searching for a needle in a haystack."

Spencer argued.

"Maybe so. But first thing tomorrow morning, I'm headed across the street." Rachel nodded in an eastward direction.

"The library." Amber confirmed.

"Meet me there at noon, and everybody stay together." Rachel's tone was tense. Fear and dread threatened to overtake her as she clasped her hands together at her waist, her knuckles turning white.

She stood up from her chair and swung her purse over her shoulder. Then she searched the eyes of all of them and made a spine-chilling announcement.

"If Ryan Banks was a living person at one time, it would mean that his ghost might have actually made contact through the Ouija board. But if the story of Ryan Banks proves to be false, then it could only mean that not only is the spirit a liar, but it's now haunting us all."

# *Eleven*

Rachel arrived at the library an hour earlier than the others. She was eager to get started digging through old newspaper files, and she had already devised a plan to keep the Ouija board incidents a secret from campus administration and anybody who might start asking questions. Nobody needed to know about the game's disturbing effects on the students. Even though she considered moving out of Kendall Hall, how would she explain her reasons to the Housing Department? Most of the dorms were completely full, and in order to switch rooms, she knew that she would have to present a valid reason. Offering an excuse of having bad dreams or being haunted by a Ouija Board spirit wouldn't fly. For all she knew, there were only six of them being targeted by the spirit. She was unaware of the paranoia caused to the rest of the students who had witnessed the angry spirit's force just days before.

Rachel parked her car outside the side entrance of the building. She walked down the sidewalk and skipped up the steps leading to the library's front entrance. As she neared the glass doors, she saw a familiar face. A young man about twentyish sat at a desk just a few feet inside the door. He stared down at an open book lying flat on the table in front of him. He appeared to be deeply engrossed in its contents as he slowly flipped the pages one at a time, often pausing to study what looked like pictures from a distance.

Then just as Rachel pulled the door open, a memory flashed before her. Her recollection of the young man replayed into a vivid storyline of mental images as she quietly glided past him and hurried to the opposite side of the room. She remembered him now, and a creepy uncomfortable sensation swept over her. He was the guy who had survived a horrific motorcycle accident just the year before, but he had never been quite the same since that day.

It happened early one morning before first period class on the high school campus. He and a buddy made a near fatal error in judgement when they climbed onto a motorcycle without bothering to strap on a helmet.

Matt Henley was driving as the two daredevils raced up and down the parking lot while their classmates watched and cheered them on. It was risky fun until the bike accelerated over a speed bump sending Drew Mathis flying into the air. He landed on his back as his head bounced off the asphalt, splitting his skull in half and exposing a portion of his brain.

At that moment, the lights went out for Drew and didn't come back on until three months later when he awakened from a coma. Once a friendly kid with a pleasant disposition, he was now more of an introvert who was easily agitated and prone to hostile outbursts. Although he had survived, the life altering accident had left him with a bizarre new identity that others found creepy and unnerving.

Suddenly Drew glanced up as Rachel passed. She let out a short gasp when the two of them made eye contact and walked faster toward the media room. She pushed open the door leading into the room and darted between two rows of metal filing cabinets. She then peered around the corner, her eyes searching madly around the room making sure that he had not followed her.

He was nowhere to be seen. She peered past the glass windows and to the area where he had been sitting just seconds before. Gone. He was now gone. She waited a few more seconds. If he was nearby, she would see him. But three minutes passed, and she concluded that he must have left the building.

Rachel tilted her head back and let out a long sigh. She then straightened her shirt and adjusted her purse strap on her shoulder. She slowly began to move away from the back of the files when all of a sudden Drew Mathis dashed in front of her, blocking her exit. She screamed but quickly covered her mouth as if it would discourage curious eyes and ears from coming to investigate. Rachel didn't want any trouble with Drew

Mathis, but she also didn't want to attract attention from the librarian or any other students. She felt like a private investigator. A paranormal private investigator. And it worried her. What would people think? *If she was tagged with that title, she would definitely be sent to the nut house.*

Drew immediately began boxing her in as he moved closer to her, pushing her backwards toward the wall. His eyes looked sunken, and his skin was a light grey. She could see part of the scar on his forehead where his head had been sewn back together.

"Drew, what do you want?" Rachel was firm, her voice strong and confident, but deep down her insides were shaking like hell.

Drew remained quiet. He stared at the ground and fidgeted with his front pockets.

"Drew, what are you doing? I need to go now. Let me pass." Rachel pressed.

Drew began to snap his left fingers in the air while staring at her as if he was keeping in tune with a musical score. His eyes looked vacant for a moment and then fluttered as he spoke in broken sentences. "You know—

that—I have. You know that I—like you. A lot. I like—you a lot."

Rachel watched for any movement of Drew's right hand that was still shoved inside his pants pocket and hidden from view. Her stomach churned as she eyed the scar on his forehead again. And for a second, she felt as if she might vomit. *Did he have a gun?* Her heart was racing, and her eyes were now wide open moving back and forth from his hands to his face. She struggled to stay calm, not wanting to show fear or let him know that he had the best of her.

"Drew, that's so sweet of you. Can we talk another time? I need to go." Rachel's attempt to be sweet and accommodating did no good. There was no point in trying to reason with him because that part of his brain no longer connected in ways that were vital to his social skills.

"No." Drew swung his right hand around, exposing the blade of a knife. He traced the razor sharp blade against a stack of books sitting on top of the cabinet, determined to hold her hostage.

"I've liked you a long time, Rachel. Why—don't—

you like me back?" He stuttered. Spit pockets formed in the corners of his mouth. He made a slurping noise and swallowed as his eyes roamed the length of her body.

Rachel's eyes began to tear up. Her chest was hurting now as if she was having a heart attack, and she felt that she might lose her breath at any moment. She stared in horror at the blade of the knife, now just inches away from reaching her throat if Drew decided to lash out.

Seconds seemed like hours as she stood there facing a danger she had never known. Drew Mathis was creepy, but he had never been dangerous. Until now. Rachel's body trembled as she listened to him snap his fingers. The bottom of her legs were now shaking so hard that she was afraid they might buckle at any moment.

Then she tried once more to show dominance over him. She reasoned that if she screamed and scared him, he might stab her for sure, but if she stood there and did nothing, he might actually kill her anyway. She had to be bold, but she was afraid to take her eyes off him. If only somebody would walk into the media room and rescue her. *Somebody. Anybody.*

Then in one brave and bold move, Rachel nonchalantly stepped forward into Drew's personal space and ordered him to step aside.

"Drew, get the hell out of my way!" She shouted, stressing each word with a cold and harsh tone as she glared at him with fierce eyes.

Drew was shocked by Rachel's sudden bravery. His face dropped, and his mouth fell slightly open. Rachel had made an aggressive move that countered him and stole his control. But it saved her life.

She stepped three feet away from him and broke into a run, but just as she reached the door, Nate slammed head-on into her.

"Hey—What's the rush?! I thought I saw your car outside." Nate looked puzzled as he watched Drew rush past the two of them and out the door.

He looked back at Rachel now fighting back tears. "What the hell? What's wrong? Do you know that guy?"

Rachel nodded. "Yeah, he's messed up."

Nate responded with a humorless laugh. "What do you mean?"

Rachel rubbed her eyes, smearing mascara down her cheek. She then reached forward and hugged Nate, wrapping her arms tight around him. Her voice was a frantic whisper. "That guy pulled a knife on me."

"No way! Just now? He did that now?" Nate asked with alarm. He pulled Rachel away and examined her. "That's insane. We need to stop that bastard. Or get security over here. You need to tell Officer Bobby about that!"

Rachel took several deep breaths. "He had a bad accident a couple of years ago. Messed him up."

"No shit, but that's screwed up. You need to report it." Nate wasn't going to let Rachel dismiss the guy's assault because of some medical condition.

Rachel nodded and used both hands to sweep tears away from her cheeks.

"It's that damn board. Nothing but bad luck. And weird shit keeps happening."

"Maybe. But when we leave here, I want you to talk to Officer Bobby. He needs to know about that crazy ass dude."

"I will." Rachel agreed.

"Okay, I'm going with you."

Rachel nodded. "Where are the others?"

Nate turned and looked behind him just as Josie, Amber, and Stephanie passed the front desk. Spencer followed behind them. Nate pointed toward the group. "There they are. Right on time."

Josie rushed to Rachel's side, terror in her eyes and her body noticeably shaken.

"Hey, did you see that crazy guy who just ran out of here? He had blood all over him."

"What?! Who?!" Rachel cried out. Her immediate thought was that Drew had stabbed someone outside the library.

"Yeah, he just slashed his wrists." Spencer announced as the sound of an ambulance siren echoed outside the library's front door.

# Twelve

"Jesus Christ, man. Are you shitting me?" Nate exclaimed with horror.

"Dude, that guy just tried to cut me. If Nate hadn't come in the library when he did, I might be dead now." Rachel leaned forward and bent over, placing her hands on her knees. She felt nauseous again and fought a sudden urge to vomit, but coughed instead.

"Oh my god, are you okay?" Josie placed her hand on Rachel's back.

Rachel took a deep breath. "Let's get the hell out of

here."

"Were you able to find out anything?" Stephanie asked as they hurriedly left the area.

Rachel turned and looked back at Stephanie in surprise. She shook her head and then rolled her eyes. *Was anybody aware that she almost got slashed to hell by some maniac in the library?*

"Let's head over to campus security in a couple of hours. I want to ask Mr. Bobby if he knows anything." Josie suggested.

Rachel held her stomach as Nate followed by her side. No one disagreed with Josie. Their silence was unanimous approval to interview the well-liked campus police officer who had patrolled the college's streets for more than a decade.

The six of them hung out at the Student Activity Building until they observed the last emergency vehicle leave the area where Drew Mathis had been strapped down to a gurney and loaded in an ambulance. The group stood near the windows watching the scene while listening to Rachel recount her two minutes of horror, trapped between the file cabinets and fearing for her life before the disturbed man slashed his wrists on the front steps of the library.

Spencer pushed the door open. They walked down the sidewalk to the campus police department to meet Officer Bobby Edwards, a favorite among many of the students at Riverside College. A bachelor in his early thirties who still lived at home, Bobby got along well with the young adults and quickly became friends with many who seemed to adopt him as an older brother or uncle.

Although he was an imposing 6'4", 265 pound man, his demeanor and kind disposition overshadowed an otherwise intimidating stature unless it was nightfall and past curfew. Officer Bobby had scared more than a few students during his tenure. Young adults often got locked out of their dorms, and the only available option was climbing through a ground floor window. Anyone who found themselves standing in the direct path of Officer Bobby's headlights as he circled the dorm buildings was as good as caught in spite of every attempt to hide behind the shrubbery or lay face down under the starry midnight sky. And nobody dared to awaken Ms. Ruth at Kendall Hall if it was past curfew. Facing a fine and a verbal lashing from Officer Bobby was less harsh than the consequences of pissing off the 'Ole Lady' on the first floor.

Josie rushed past Spencer so that she could lead the group down the sidewalk toward campus security. She paused at the front entrance and waited for Stephanie and Amber to catch up as the rest of the group fell in behind her. She slowly pushed the door open and walked inside a narrow hall leading to several offices. The building smelled of pine sol, and the inside temperature was a cool sixty-eight degrees Fahrenheit. Josie seemed to know her way around the place as she made her way down the hall to the last door on the right.

"Knock, knock. Mr. Bobby? Are you busy?" Josie called out in a hushed tone. She slowly looked around the open door and peered inside where Bobby sat at his small metal desk scribbling on a piece of paper. He instantly recognized Josie's voice and glanced toward the door.

"Hey, Josie!" Officer Bobby was his usual friendly self.

"Hey, Mr. Bobby. Have you got a minute?" Josie stepped inside and motioned for Nate and the others to follow. Officer Bobby laid his pen down and started to stand up from his chair.

"Sure. Sure, I do. What brings you over?" Officer Bobby moved around to the front of the desk and sat down on the corner facing the group.

"Mr. Bobby, we're doing a little investigating and wanted to ask you a few questions."

Bobby laughed. "Okay. Well, first tell me who your friends are."

"Oh gosh, of course." Josie said in an apologetic tone and indicated who each person was by pointing them out as she called each of their names. "This is Rachel Thomas. Amber Simmons. Stephanie Baker. Spencer Gordon. And Nate Larson."

Officer Bobby Edwards grinned and nodded 'hello' to the group then looked back at Josie.

Josie paused until Officer Bobby gave her an

inquisitive look, inviting her to speak.

"Mr. Bobby, have you ever heard of a student committing suicide here? Like a few years ago?"

Officer Bobby Edwards made a face, squeezing his eyebrows together and smacking his lips shut as if he was deep in thought. He rubbed his hands, palms down against his legs while leaning forward. Goosebumps crawled up his arms, and a few seconds passed before he spoke.

Nate studied Bobby's reaction and began to formulate an opinion. He decided that the officer knew something that he didn't want to talk about.

Although Bobby was a professed skeptic of anything paranormal or spooky, he couldn't deny feeling creeped out by Josie's inquiry. There was no way for her to know, but this wasn't the first time that he had been confronted with these questions.

As Josie waited for Bobby's response, she began to feel uncomfortable. She sensed that he was about to tell her something horrific or maybe she had opened a can of worms that she shouldn't have. Her heart began to beat faster, and she felt feverish.

Bobby looked up and scanned the faces of everyone there. His tone was convincing and carried a subtle warning that suggested they shouldn't probe any further.

"As far as I know, no one has ever killed themselves on this campus." Bobby stood tall and erect, and folded his arms across his chest.

An unnerving silence followed his response. It didn't make sense. Nate looked at him with suspicious eyes and didn't believe a word of what he said or more importantly, what he wasn't saying. Everyone felt uneasy, but Officer Bobby managed to keep his sudden anxiety hidden from the group.

Josie hesitated and then finally spit out her words. "You mean—you mean, you never heard anything either?"

Chills crept down her spine as she locked eyes with Officer Bobby. Not one of them moved an inch from where they were standing, their feet nailed to the floor.

"Have you kids been playing with that talking board game?" Bobby looked at the group through squinted eyes.

Nate stepped back from the door's entrance. Fear

enveloped his body like a fist slamming into his face. He felt his entire body begin to tingle with a creepiness that wouldn't go away. He shoved his hands in his front pants pocket.

Rachel stepped forward and touched Nate's arm. She offered him a concealed but reassuring squeeze as she brushed past him and faced Officer Bobby.

"You mean a Ouija board? Yes, sir."

Bobby shook his head and leaned back. "I was hoping this wouldn't happen again."

"What do you mean?" Rachel pressed, pretending not to know anything about the board's reputation.

"Every year, kids bring those darn things on campus. It just stirs things up." Bobby rubbed his forehead.

"Stirs up what things, Mr. Bobby?" Josie followed Rachel's lead.

"A couple years ago, a rumor got started around campus after a few kids got to playing with one of those boards. They claimed that they contacted a spirit who committed suicide in the courtyard over at Eastside Hall." Bobby pointed his thumb in the direction of the infamous dorm.

"All this silly crap got in these kid's heads." Bobby said with a frown.

Josie turned and looked at the others with a 'oh my god, what now' expression. No one said a word for what seemed like hours. Then finally Amber broke the silence.

"So this has happened before. And nobody has ever committed suicide here? A kid who played baseball?" Amber was shocked by the new revelation, especially since she had spoken to Ryan Banks herself through the board. She believed that the spirit was real. After all, she knew him. He had become her friend.

Bobby shook his head. "No one. It's just a story."

"Ryan Banks. His name is Ryan Banks." Amber stated with agitation, her voice rising.

"I've worked here for more than ten years. Nothing like that has happened. And I don't know any kid who has died here by the name of Ryan Banks. This is all a fabricated story." Bobby became annoyed and stood up.

Amber turned and walked out with Stephanie following fast behind her.

The rest of the group stood frozen in place, wide eyed

and staring at Officer Bobby in complete bewilderment. It was as if they had imagined it all, but they had not. Each and every one of them, including the other thirty-four students who were present at the music hall that night during the Ouija game, witnessed the windows almost shattering and Nate Larson's collapse. There was no way that had been imagined.

Rachel no longer wanted to disclose anything else to Officer Bobby. She gave Josie a nudge.

"We better get going, Josie." Rachel half-smiled at Officer Bobby and mouthed the words 'thank you'.

"Hey, thanks, Mr. Bobby. We'll see you around." Josie turned and followed the others out the door, but just as they reached the exit, Officer Bobby called out and halted them before Nate's foot crossed the door's threshold.

"You kids need to leave that board game alone. Do you hear me? Leave it alone." His tone carried an unmistakable warning as he studied them with a penetrating scowl.

Josie slowed and turned to look back over her shoulder as she continued to follow Rachel. "Yes, sir."

Josie answered in a low tone that was barely above a whisper just before the door slammed behind her.

As the two girls joined Nate and Spencer on the sidewalk, Rachel noticed Amber running toward Kendall Hall.

"Hey, where's Amber going?" Rachel asked.

"I don't know. Maybe she got spooked." Spencer joked.

Nate dissed Spencer's comment under his breath and silently confessed to himself that there were plenty of reasons to be spooked about the current events with the Ouija board. He gave Rachel and Josie a sideways look and shrugged.

"Who knows? She just said that she would catch us later." Nate added, but his tone suggested the same thing that Rachel was thinking.

Rachel watched her from a distance as she entered the front door to Kendall Hall. That weird feeling was coming back stronger than ever before. That gut feeling that told her something wasn't as it seemed, and she just couldn't shake it no matter how hard she tried. She didn't trust Amber. She knew that Amber was going to keep messing with a spiritual world that she wasn't prepared to confront.

Ryan Banks was an immortal entity that had never walked the earth in a human body. He was a fictional character masquerading as an earthbound spirit, but he had a much more sinister motive. If Amber Simmons was still summoning the dark entity as Rachel suspected that she was, it would only be a matter of time before the spirit would invade her mind completely. She was becoming obsessed with the board, opening a portal for Ryan Banks to enter. And once the spirit was here, all hell on earth would be unleashed.

# Thirteen

Rachel walked steadfast toward Kendall Hall. Her contact lenses were glued to her eyeballs, and her right knee began to ache from the previous day's injury at cheer practice when she slipped in damp grass and fell to the ground. A grass stain and a black and blue bruise painted the front of her kneecap now. Although the bruise was hidden by her Gloria Vanderbilt designer jeans, her injury was evident by a slight limp in her stride. She grimaced as the denim material brushed against the scratches on her knee.

Rachel needed a break, and she wanted to go home

for a couple of nights. But just as she turned to tell the others 'goodbye', Nate walked up to her and reached out, taking her by the arm.

"Rachel, wait up!" Nate looked down at Rachel's leg as she held her heel slightly off the ground. Then he pointed at her knee and waited for her to answer.

"I fell yesterday at cheer." Rachel said.

"I didn't notice you limping until now." Nate replied with raised eyebrows.

"I know. It starts hurting after I've been on it awhile." Rachel turned away and stepped forward, but Nate stopped her again.

"Wait." Nate didn't want Rachel to leave. Although he was beginning to like her, he also couldn't deny that he was more than a little paranoid to be alone since the Ouija nightmare had started. And he wanted answers as much as she did.

Spencer walked past the two of them. "I'll catch you guys later. I'm going back to the dorm and watch some horror." He mocked and covered his mouth as he busted out in obnoxious laughter. Rachel turned and rolled her eyes at Spencer.

"You aren't going to take that cop's word for it, are you? We need to talk to someone else." Nate spoke as if he was ready to assume a lead role as detective, his tone serious and determined.

Rachel shrugged and then shook her head once. "No, I think you're right."

"Let's interview one of the baseball coaches. If Ryan Banks played baseball here and committed suicide, one of the coaches should know about him." Nate suggested.

"I agree." Rachel turned to Josie who was now walking up to Nate's side.

Josie heard Nate's suggestion as she was approaching and gave Rachel a thumbs up. "Yep, and I know which one we need to talk to."

"Really, who?" Rachel asked.

"Coach Scott." Josie said.

"Coach Scott? Why him?" Nate asked.

"I think he's been here longer than anyone else." Josie said with confidence.

"How do you know?" Rachel asked, wondering how Josie had suddenly become so knowledgeable about the tenure of Riverside's faculty.

"I don't, but it's a starting point. And he's the only coach I've seen around campus." Josie snorted.

Rachel and Nate laughed at the same time.

"Alright then, Sherlock. We'll start there." Rachel said.

"Let's go. His house is two blocks over on the west side of the campus. If we're lucky, we might catch him at home." Josie turned and motioned for the other two to follow.

Rachel sighed as she fell in behind Josie, slowly limping along. Nate studied the ground with an undetected grin of satisfaction then glanced over at Rachel and admired her thick and shiny brunette tresses. He offered his arm for her to lean on, and Rachel accepted without hesitation.

"Do you think Officer Bobby is hiding something?" Rachel was becoming more and more surprised by Josie's interest in the investigation. She figured that Josie would accept Bobby's statements, not rebuke them and offer to lead the hunt for Ryan Banks' true identity.

Josie frowned. "I don't know, but I'm not satisfied with what he told us."

Rachel and Nate looked at each other and answered at the same time.

"Neither am I."

Amber wasted no time as she rushed past Stephanie toward Kendall Hall. She now reasoned that the campus dorm was the best location for summoning the spirit of Ryan Banks since Bobby Edwards had just given her the confirmation she had secretly been searching for. The Ouija spirit had been around for a long time. He wasn't someone new, and Amber was now more curious than ever about the spirit's identity and its reason for being there. She wasn't the type to leave well enough alone. She had become too sucked into the mystery and the excitement of its dangerous lure.

She didn't slow down as she neared the front entrance, cutting across the grass instead of using the sidewalk. She then darted through the door and skipped two steps at a time when she reached the stairs leading to the second floor. She heard Stephanie call out in the distance but ignored her as she continued down the hall to the last door on the right.

She closed the door behind her and locked it. Then she walked over to the closet and pushed the sliding door to the left until it was completely open. She stood on her tiptoes and ran her hand along the top wooden shelf as she felt for the Ouija box that she had carefully hidden out of sight. Her fingertips searched near the back of the shelf and finally touched the corner of the box. She inched her fingers closer, grabbing onto its edge. She pulled it toward her and then managed to slide the box a few inches closer until she was able to pick it up.

She stepped back and rested on her heels as she looked down at the box in her hands. She stared at the picture of the Ouija board on the outside cardboard cover and slid her hand across the top, examining the picture of the planchette as if it was one of those 'magic eye' pictures that changed every time it moved from one angle to the next.

She wondered how something that appeared to be nothing more than a board made of wood particle chips could turn from a game of magic and make-believe to a game of malice and malevolent spirits. Nothing made sense anymore. But in spite of the warnings and the dangers she had seen firsthand, she found herself opening the box again as she sat down in the center of the floor.

It had been three days since she had contacted the Ouija spirit. Even though she and Stephanie had experienced the spirit's fury weeks before when it sent the two of them racing down the fire escape, she couldn't deny how much she missed talking to her invisible friend. She was infatuated by his attentiveness and his ability to tell her things that only a supernatural being could know. She was sucked into its allure like a cult member, brainwashed and braindead. But the past three days, she had left it alone. She was waiting to find out if Ryan Banks was a myth or a truth that the college didn't want known. Maybe his death had brought the college bad publicity? Maybe there were pieces of the puzzle that had not been discovered? Or maybe Ryan Banks's death was a deeply buried secret that Bobby Edwards was determined to keep hidden. She asked herself the same questions that the others mulled over, but so far Rachel had uncovered nothing that persuaded her to abandon the game. She situated the board on her lap and then placed the planchette in the center.

"Ryan, are you here? It's me. Amber. I need to talk to you." Amber felt a slight vibration as her fingertips gently brushed the edge of the planchette. Then she held her breath and watched it move to the upper left corner.

*YES.*

# Fourteen

The planchette zipped back and forth across the alphabet as it spelled out words. Words that weren't making sense at first.

N-E-W-S. M-E-E-T.

"News? Meet? I don't understand, Ryan. Do you mean that I should meet someone?" Amber watched the board as if she thought the spirit was suddenly going to climb out.

The planchette raced to the upper right corner.

*NO.*

Amber continued to follow the planchette in a figure

eight movement around the board. Her fingertips had little control once the spirit took over. "Okay." She whispered.

Amber remained quiet for a few seconds. Then a sudden flash of intuition burst forth. "Oh, you mean, Officer Bobby?"

The planchette almost flew off the board but landed in the upper left corner.

*YES.*

Amber gasped and felt the urge to cough. Her heart skipped a beat.

"You knew that we met Officer Bobby today?"

*YES.*

L-I-A-R.

"Liar? Who? I don't understand."

*YES.*

B-O-B-B-Y.

Amber got a chill, and moved her hands away from the planchette for a moment. She rubbed her arms and looked around the room as if she was searching for the entity. Expecting him to show himself at any minute. Then she took a breath and placed her fingertips back on the planchette.

Amber mumbled. "The spirit must have been there. You were there?"

*YES.*

S-A-D.

Amber watched as the spirit continued to spell words. She hesitated to give the spirit anymore promptings and waited instead to see how much it would disclose.

M-U-R-D-E-R-E-R

S-P-E-N-C-E-R

H-I-D-E.

Amber's skin turned ice cold. She watched in utter horror as the planchette spelled out one word at a time, leaving her to decode a message that she feared was an omen.

"Ryan, you're scaring me. Officer Bobby said that you're not real." Amber's skin tingled, and her eyes began to water.

The planchette raced across the board. Amber gasped as it darted to the upper left corner.

*YES.*

I-A-M.

Amber chose to ignore the spirit's message as she continued to ask it questions.

"But were you a real person?"

*YES.*

N-O-O-N-E C-A-N H-E-L-P N-O-W.

Amber screamed and jerked back. She fell backwards against the wall with her hand covering her mouth. She took deep breaths and then leaned forward and placed her hands back on the board.

The spirit quickly returned, racing across the alphabet.

I-P-R-O-T-E-C-T-Y-O-U.

Amber's mouth hung open. "You protect me?"

*YES.*

A-C-C-I-D-E-N-T.

H-U-R-T. S-P-E-N-C-E-R.

Amber heard familiar footsteps walking fast toward the door. In one swift move, she slid the planchette down to the bottom of the board and whispered aloud.

"Goodbye, Ryan."

She then jumped up, slammed the board back in its box and flung it to the back of the closet shelf just as

Stephanie inserted her key in the door. As she entered the room, Amber eased the closet door shut behind her and wiped any trace of deceit from her face as she greeted her friend with a nonchalant 'hello'.

Josie stepped up on the front porch of Coach Randall Scott's home. She pushed the round circular button next to the brick entrance and waited as the doorbell remitted a long, singular chime throughout the house. Rachel noticed two ferns situated on the corners of the porch and a hand shovel still covered in the potting soil that was used to cover the plants. A couple of minutes passed, and no one answered the door.

"I don't think anybody's here." Rachel stood on her tiptoes and peered through the front door window.

Josie frowned. "Yeah, I guess not."

Just then the sharp buzzing of a lawnmower's engine sounded from the back of the house as the mower's pulley was yanked back and forth. Sounds of frustration came next as the coach shouted obscenities, unaware that anyone could hear him.

The three of them looked at each other, and Nate lifted his index finger in the air and pointed to the back of the house. Josie jumped off the porch and made a quick dash for the backyard with Rachel and Nate following close behind. Just as they turned the corner of the house, they saw the coach bent over the mower and meddling with a cable. He jerked upright as he caught a glimpse of them coming around the corner.

"Hey, Coach Scott." Josie said with a slight nervous tone. She greeted the esteemed college baseball coach with a degree of shyness that was uncommon for her in most situations, but this was different. She was about to ask the coach to validate the story of Ryan Banks, and she hoped that he didn't want to know why she was inquiring. How would she tell him that Ryan Banks was a Ouija board spirit?

The coach stepped back from the mower and wiped his brow. He looked at the three of them with curiosity. "Yes, what can I do for you?"

Josie extended her hand in an awkward handshake.

"My name is Josie Norton, and these are my friends, Nate Larson and Rachel Thomas. We're trying to find out about a student who died here. A kid who committed suicide."

The coach pursed his lips and looked away as if he was deep in thought then shook his head.

"You don't remember ever hearing about that?" Rachel asked.

"Who was the kid?" The coach cocked his head to the side and looked at Rachel.

"His name was Ryan Banks."

"Ryan Banks." The coach repeated his name and glanced down at the ground, shaking his head.

"No, I don't guess I've ever heard of anybody by that name. And what did you say happened to him?" Coach Scott glanced over at Josie.

"He committed suicide. We heard that he was a baseball player on campus." Josie shoved her hands in her front pants pockets.

"I've never heard of him. If that happened, it must have happened before I came here. And I've been here for fifteen years." The coach studied Josie. He was now focused on her and forgot about the frustrating lawnmower that wouldn't start.

"Now tell me again. Why are you kids looking into this?" Coach Scott rested his left hand on his hip.

All three of them swallowed hard at the same time. Josie hesitated to answer. No one had told the coach why they were 'looking into this', and no one really wanted to answer that question. Rachel hoped Josie wouldn't tell him the truth.

"Oh, I was working on a research paper about suicide on college campuses and heard that it happened here at Riverside." Josie lied.

The coach shook his head and offered an apologetic smile. "Okay, sorry I couldn't help you." The coach turned back to his mower and began to tug on the starter cable again.

"Yes, sir. Thank you." Josie turned and motioned with an eye gesture for Nate and Rachel to follow her.

As she walked away, the coach watched the three of them and silently considered the reasons for their inquiry. For a brief blip in time, he wondered if there was any truth to the story or existence of Ryan Banks, but as he reached for the mower pulley, the consideration became an afterthought as he jerked the cord hard and fast. The mower's engine cranked and vibrated with a loud and steady buzz.

# Fifteen

## Eastside Hall, dark thirty...

Spencer Gordon hung his bath towel on the metal wall rack after toweling off from a much needed hot shower. He then flipped the light switch off and made his way to the small sitting area next to his bed.

He reached down and tossed a metal fork aside as he grabbed the last bite of french fries leftover from lunch. He shoved them in his mouth and picked up a VHS movie box. He flipped open the cover of *Friday the 13th: Jason Lives* and found it empty. He then pushed the play button on the VHS/VCR player. The movie picked up where he had paused the VHS tape hours before after leaving the rest of the group to continue their research of Ryan Banks.

The terrifying image of Jason Voorhees flashed onto the 19-inch television screen as he raised the machete into the air and then brought it down in one hard, slashing move that slit the face of his victim in half. Spencer was only slightly grossed out by the lead character's horror. He had seen every movie to date in the Friday the 13th franchise, but this was his favorite, especially the beginning of the movie when Jason's grave is desecrated. Spencer shook his head and mumbled to himself that 'they should have known better' than to disturb the gory murderer's resting place, but the opening scene set the tone for the next 90 minutes as the resurrected, worm infested killer engaged in multiple bloody orgies.

He leaned back and propped his hands behind his head. The spine tingling music in the movie began to intensify causing Spencer to clasp his hands tighter in a bone crushing lock. He watched Jason snap the electrical wires connected to an RV inhabited by a couple of teenage fornicators.

Then without warning, Spencer felt a wave of cold air brush across his face. He ran his fingers through his messy wet hair and let out a sigh as he stared at the television screen.

The male actor declared it was 'time to go' as his eyes searched past the foggy trees ahead of him and then announced that 'someone was out there'. Spencer's thoughts filled with the recent memory of Nate's Ouija scare as he watched the resurrected zombie of Jason Voorhees on the screen, a walking dead killer brought back to life by a bolt of lightning.

*Was the Ouija board a hoax? Had Nate simply been a participant in a dramatically planned parlor trick?* Then without any warning or explanation at all, the distinct sound of laughter came forth just inches from Spencer's ear.

He jerked around, his body lifting off the seat of the chair as his heart skipped a beat. He turned his head from side to side as he surveyed the small dorm room for any hidden intruders, but he saw no one. He leaned over the side of the chair and looked behind him. Nothing.

Screams came from the television as Jason slammed a teenage girl from side to side inside the RV's claustrophobic sized restroom. Then it came again, but this time it was louder and wicked. A hoarse, deep laugh accompanied by a strange fluttering noise that sounded like birds taking flight.

"Hey, who's there? You pricks can come out now. You ain't funny." Spencer ordered. His voice was loud, but his insides were churning like the onset of a bad stomach virus. He reached over and pressed the pause button on the VHS remote.

Time seemed to pass in slow motion as he put the remote back down on the small cocktail table in front of him and reached for the plate piled with leftover bread crumbs and empty food wrappers. But just as he touched the plate's edge, the metal fork that he had left there lifted into mid-air and sailed across the room with a force so violent it buried its four prongs into the sheet rock wall.

Spencer fell backwards as a malevolent force slammed against him, knocking him off his feet. The plate flew into the air and then dropped to the floor, scattering leftovers everywhere as his lower back made contact with the edge of the table. He yelled out in pain as tears burst forth and rolled over his eyelids. He gasped and coughed, but the spirit's laughter turned to whispers as it taunted him and urged him to do its bidding.

*Get Rachel first, and kill them all. Kill them now.*

Spencer squeezed his eyes open and shut. He panted in a desperate attempt to breathe as the stabbing pains seared deep within his thoracic cavity. He managed to roll over on his stomach and then dragged his body across the floor, using his arms to pull himself forward. His heart beat hard and fast as saliva pooled in his mouth, and he fought the urge to vomit.

He told himself that this was not happening to him. He was an atheist. Spirits weren't real. But it *was* happening, and he had to get out of there. He grunted and spit each time he exhaled. Finally, he was able to crawl across the floor until he made it to the door. Then he gritted his teeth and took a painful, deep breath as he hoisted himself up. He grabbed the doorknob and yanked it open. As he collapsed against the hard tile floor, his head slammed face first, and the tender soft skin of his right eyebrow sliced open. Spencer Gordon now laid motionless as a trickle of blood formed a puddle underneath his cheek.

Nate skipped up the steps toward Spencer's room. He had already made up his mind to move his things back home during the Thanksgiving holidays. He couldn't talk himself back into sleeping in his own dorm room, and he didn't want to explain his reasons to anybody who might ask. Even though he was embarrassed by his need to stay with someone, he wasn't ready to proclaim macho status and a return to the alpha male circle. If the rest of the gang wanted to label him a "sissy", then so be it.

He turned the corner at the top of the stairs and stopped dead still. His heart felt as if it dropped to the floor, and his mouth fell open at the sight of Spencer Gordon laying in the doorway of his dorm room, the open door resting against his body as if he was a doorstop. A split second later, Nate's feet became light as he raced forward to the end of the hall. The rubber soles of his sneakers squeaked against the floor as he came to an abrupt halt in front of Spencer. He leaned down and touched his shoulder.

"Spence! Spence! Can you hear me?" Nate was frantic.

"Help! Somebody help!" Nate yelled, his voice bounced off the walls and reverberated into an echo down the stairs. Beads of sweat popped out on his forehead as he jumped up and banged on doors on the opposite side of the hall. He then raced back to Spencer's side and knelt down again beside him.

"Spencer. Answer me." Nate covered his mouth with one hand. His eyes began to water, and he wanted so desperately to cry. He was frantic as he tapped Spencer's back, repeatedly calling out to him. He then placed his index and middle finger on Spencer's neck and felt for a pulse, but just as he applied pressure, a low grunt escaped from Spencer's lips. Nate jerked back.

"Oh, thank Jesus! It's gonna be okay, man." Nate reassured Spencer.

A door opened across the hall. "Oh wow, what

happened?" The neighbor asked, rubbing his hands through a headful of sandy colored hair.

"I don't know. I just found him. Go get somebody! Hurry!" Nate was near screaming now.

The neighbor rushed down the stairs and bolted through the front door. Just as he stepped outside on the front sidewalk of Eastside Hall, he saw the familiar headlights of Officer Bobby Edwards as he drove along the main campus road. He rushed out to the edge of the street and waved his hands in the air, motioning for the officer to stop. As Officer Bobby approached, he slowed the car and rolled down the window as the guy ran to the driver's side door.

"Come quick. Somebody--is hurt. They're lying--in the floor on--the 2$^{nd}$ floor." The neighbor stuttered through heavy breathing.

Officer Bobby looked to the right with one eyebrow cocked as he peered out the front windshield of his car.

"At Eastside?" He pointed to the dorm ahead.

"Yes, Sir. Hurry." The kid moved back as the officer slammed the car in drive and pulled forward into an empty parking space at the front of the dorm building.

Officer Bobby released the door handle and pushed it open with his foot. He climbed out of the vehicle with the radio mic glued to his hand as he called the dispatcher.

"Central, we need an ambulance dispatched to Eastside Hall at Riverside. Severity of injury is unknown. Stand by." The officer then turned back to Spencer's neighbor.

"What's your name?" Officer Bobby glanced down at the short, stocky male.

"My name is Grant Kirk. I live across the hall." The freshman baseball player looked up at the tall officer.

"You know what happened?" Bobby asked in a tone that signaled an investigation was forthcoming.

"No, another dude banged on my door and called for help." Grant quickly eliminated himself from further questioning.

Bobby ran up the sidewalk and bolted up the stairs as he passed through the front door. He climbed two steps at a time until he reached the hall where Spencer now lay still but with his eyes open. He rolled his head to the right and peered up at the officer as Bobby bent down to examine the severity of Spencer's bloody lanced eye.

"What's your name, son?" Officer Bobby remembered Spencer's face from the day Josie had brought him by the office, but he couldn't remember his name. He looked at the wound and guessed that he would need a few stitches above his right brow.

"Spencer Gordon." He mumbled.

"Ok, Spencer. Just lay still. An ambulance is on the way. Do you remember how you ended up here?" Officer Bobby remained in a kneeled position by Spencer's side.

Spencer responded with slurred speech. "Yeah---I fell inside my room and hit the edge of a table. I—I landed so hard that it knocked the breath out of me." He winced with pain as he paused to take a deep breath.

"How did you end up in the doorway?" Bobby wondered if Spencer had been assaulted.

"I- I crawled to the door, but I fell and—

Spencer mumbled a little louder but then paused. His mouth was pressed against the floor and drool was dripping from his lips. He wanted the ambulance there yesterday. The right side of his face was covered in blood, and his eye was irritated and itchy as blood pooled into the socket.

Just then Bobby heard the ambulance pull around to the front entrance. Emergency personnel was out of the vehicle and in the downstairs lobby within seconds.

Officer Bobby stood up and backed away from Spencer as he heard the paramedics taking the stairs. Nate stepped forward and knelt beside Spencer again, resting against his heels.

"Hey, Spence, the paramedics are here. Just a—

Nate's attempt to inform his friend that help was on the way was cut short by Spencer's frantic whispers.

"Ryan Banks is real, dude." Spencer announced in a faint voice.

"What?" Nate asked in utter disbelief.

Spencer came again, but this time, his voice was clear. "It's real, dude. All that Ouija bullshit? It's real. Something is after us."

Nate almost fell backwards but grabbed the side of the door frame before he rocked off his heels and onto the floor. "What happened? Tell me."

Just then the paramedics turned the corner and placed

the gurney on the ground. They wasted no time and began working to get Spencer moved and out of there. Officer Bobby walked back down to the first floor where he informed the dorm mother of the incident and arranged to have the hall floor cleaned. Nate stayed back out of the way, but planned to follow the ambulance to the hospital emergency room. As the paramedics began to roll the gurney away, Nate stepped behind them.

"Hey, I'm following behind, man. I'll see you at the ER." Nate assured Spencer that he wasn't leaving his side, but Spencer was quick to oppose him.

"No. Check on Rachel first." Spencer was firm.

Nate's eyes grew big as dread overwhelmed him. He started to ask why, but before he could get the words out of his mouth, Spencer stopped him.

"Just do it, Nate. Check on her first." His tone carried a disturbing harbinger, and Nate felt his limbs go weak.

Nate managed to nod 'okay'. He watched as the paramedics rolled him out of the building while less than a quarter mile away, Rachel Thomas flipped through page after page of newspaper reels as she searched for any link to the spirit of Ryan Banks.

Rachel rushed to the back of the library. She walked between the rows of books and stopped at Section 900. She scanned shelves lined with paranormal subjects such as ghosts and hauntings until she located a couple of titles that caught her eye. She then pulled the books from the rack and quickly made her way to the media room. Just as she entered the glass doors, she unloaded her backpack onto the first empty table she saw and then grabbed a few rolls of microfilm that held the past two decades of old newspaper clippings and obituaries.

Rachel wasted no time as she sat down and opened the books searching for any clues that might help her understand *who* or *what* Ryan Banks really was. She flipped the pages to a chapter dealing with spiritual possession. Her mouth hung open as her eyes moved from left to right. She was reading fast, often skipping ahead until she found herself whispering the words aloud.

She held her ink pen between her teeth, removing it every few seconds to jot down important information. For every sentence she read, it seemed to spark another question. Then she sat back in the chair and stared straight ahead into nothingness as she contemplated what the book had just revealed, replaying the words again inside her mind.

*The dreams had not been dreams at all. Although possession was not common, it was a dangerous possibility for people using Ouija boards or other means of summoning spirits. And the spirits often take advantage of vulnerable people. People with a history of mental illness, sickness, addictions, and even children. It was not uncommon for people to experience disturbing nightmares or dreams. Spirits have been known to invade an individual's subconscious during sleep, leaving the victim unaware of the intrusion.*

"God help us." Rachel mumbled to herself. She glanced down at her watch and slowly closed the book. She pushed it aside and loaded a roll of microfilm onto the projector wheel as she flicked on the side light.

With only an hour before the library closed for the

night, Rachel hurriedly traced her finger close to the projector screen as she scanned obituaries from the past fifteen years. She moved the dial forward and then abruptly stopped, locking it in place. She leaned forward and stared at the small print facing her.

There on the screen was an entry for a woman named Margaret R. Banks. She grabbed her pen and began to jot down notes as she read the obituary aloud, her voice barely above a whisper.

> Saturday, October 28. Banks, Margaret R., 27, a Liberal Arts teacher at Riverside College died October 26, 1972 following a tragic car accident. Her body was discovered late Friday morning in the river. An investigation is ongoing by the county sheriff's department. Vaudeville Funeral Home will be handling Ms. Banks's burial, but funeral arrangements are incomplete at this time.

A cold chill swept over Rachel's body as she stared at the screen. Then the undeniable feeling of being watched overtook her, and she felt a hand brush against her head. She jerked around, her eyes darting back and forth around the room. She could have sworn that something touched her hair. She felt it move, but no one was there. In fact, there was almost no one left inside the building, and she found herself alone inside the media room again. The same room where Drew Kirk almost slit her throat just days before.

Her breathing became heavier, and her heart began to pound. She looked all around the room and past the glass windows into the other areas of the library, surveying her surroundings before silently vowing to get the hell out of there. Now.

She then stared back at the screen for a moment as she began gathering her things. *Was it a coincidence that Margaret Banks taught at Riverside and just happened to have a "R" as her middle initial? Could this be the same person? Ouija spirits were known to lie.*

Rachel scribbled down the name of the funeral home and then flipped the notebook shut. She had to find Nate and Josie and tell them what she had found. She then glanced around the room once more and jumped up. She rushed out of the media room, forgetting to turn the projector off. But just as she pushed the glass front door open, she bumped face first into Nate Larson who had been searching in earnest for her for the past twenty minutes.

Rachel dropped her notebook and pen as she slammed into Nate. "Oh my god, I was just coming to find you!" Rachel exclaimed.

Nate grabbed hold of Rachel's arms and steadied her as her ankle twisted, and she struggled to maintain her balance.

"I've been looking all over for you!" Nate was almost overwrought as he contemplated Spencer's last words to him, and Spencer was right. No one was safe anymore.

"Damn. That's the second time we've hit each other head on while coming out of the library. One of these days, we're going to have severe injuries if we keep slamming into each other like this." Rachel joked, but she really wasn't amused. She shook her head and searched Nate's eyes.

"It's Spencer. He's on his way to the hospital."

"Oh my god. What happened?"

"He had a hard fall inside his room. I just found him."

"Is he going to be okay?" Rachel's mouth hung

open. Her mind reeled with thoughts of the present danger. She wondered what it was going to take to stop the madness that was happening to them.

Nate nodded and then looked away.

Rachel studied him. "What? What is it, Nate?"

Nate stared at the ground and then raised his head back and looked up at the sky. "Something happened to Spencer. But it scared the hell out of him, and when I told him that I'd follow the ambulance to the hospital, he told me 'no'. He told me that Ryan Banks was real." Nate paused and looked at Rachel.

Rachel stared back at Nate, her eyes deadlocked with his. "Did he say anything else?"

Nate hesitated. He considered how Rachel would respond. Fear consumed all of them every single day, and this would just make it worse.

"Yeah, he demanded that I come find you. To check on you."

Rachel gasped. Her face screwed up with a look of horror. "Is he at the hospital now?"

"Probably. They left a few minutes ago."

Rachel motioned for him to follow her. "Let's get to

the car." The two of them broke into a jog as they made their way across the parking lot.

Nate called behind her. "Where are we going?"

"To the hospital first."

"Hey, why were you in such a hurry to find me? You said that---

Rachel interrupted. "I think I found something, Nate. Get in. I'll tell you on the way."

# Sixteen

## Three Hours Later...

Nate and Rachel locked their arms on each side of Spencer as they helped him out of the car at Eastside Hall. After a series of x-rays, bloodwork, and a doctor's examination, he learned that he suffered a fractured rib and a bruised spleen. The emergency room doctor told him that he'd been lucky. The fall against the corner of the table had delivered a violent blow to his back that could have caused more severe complications. A one-inch difference could have resulted in internal bleeding and the need for a life-saving operation. And as the nurse cleaned the six-inch black and blue scrape marks on his back, the doctor gave him stern instructions to rest.

Spencer walked slow, taking baby steps as they neared his dorm room. Nate stepped ahead of them and grabbed the door pushing it open, but Spencer stopped just outside the door.

"What's wrong?" Rachel waited at Spencer's side.

Spencer's face looked ashen. He shook his head and scooted his feet slowly across the floor until he was standing just inside the door's entrance. Rachel and Nate followed behind him.

His hands began to tremble as he reached out and steadied himself, placing his hands on the back of the same chair that he had been sitting in just moments before the accident. The trembling spread to the rest of his body and traveled down to his knees as he began to sweat.

"I need to sit down, man." Spencer announced through clenched teeth.

Nate and Rachel quickly gripped onto his arms and slowly moved him around to the seat of the chair. Rachel eased his body into the recliner as Nate grabbed a pillow from the bunkbed and stuffed it behind his back for extra support.

"Nate, you're staying with him, right?" Rachel asked.

"Yeah. I'll be here." Nate's tone was firm. He had no intentions of leaving Spencer alone.

Spencer wiped his hands over the length of his face. His dark brows were pressed together in a furrow as he sighed heavily and slowly blinked his eyes open and shut. The pain was subsiding, but he was weak.

Rachel and Nate responded to his anguish with an inquisitive and concerned stare that invited him to share his thoughts.

Spencer met Nate's eyes. "Did you tell her anything?" He spoke in a low, hushed tone.

Nate stared back through squinted eyes. "About what you told me?" Nate asked and then nodded.

"You told her that I heard something?" Spencer wanted a clear confirmation that Nate had informed Rachel of the danger she was in.

"I told her what you told me. That's all."

"What are you guys talking about?" Rachel pressed for them to come clean, her tone carried a slightly annoyed by their back and forth banter that sounded as if they were keeping some sort of secret.

"I think I heard the voice of Ryan Banks." Spencer looked around the room and saw the fork that had been sticking out of the wall now laying on the floor.

"And that damn fork in the floor over there flew half way across the room and landed in the wall. That's when I jumped up and fell. That caused the damn accident, man." Spencer looked at the floor where he had fallen hours before.

A sudden rush of heat swept over Rachel's body as she felt every nerve in her body come to life. "Oh. My. God. Why the hell didn't you tell us this before we brought you back here?"

"Rachel, just chill—

Nate tried to calm her, but Rachel quickly interrupted.

"Don't you understand? We're all being haunted!" Her panic filled voice was getting louder.

"Spencer, you have to tell us what you heard." Nate implored. He wasn't letting Rachel leave until Spencer told both of them exactly what happened.

Spencer looked up and searched the eyes of his friends. He paused. And then in a grave tone, he answered.

"It told me to kill."

A wave of terror washed over them, draining the color from their faces. Then Spencer brought more horror as Nate swiftly reached for the door. As he rolled his eyes away from them, he revealed what the entity had ordered him to do. In a nervous and shaking voice, he unmasked Ryan Banks's real intent.

"It told me to kill all of you."

"Oh, Hell, no! Get the hell up. We're not staying here, dude." Nate held the door open.

"Damn, Nate. Wait a minute." Rachel waved her hand in the air.

"Hell, no! We can't stay here." Nate shook his head back and forth.

"Okay, look. Spencer can't be hauled all over the

place. And do you really think that moving from one place to another is going to stop what's happening?" Rachel argued.

"Then you stay here." Nate countered.

"I'm not even supposed to be in the building, for God's sakes. This is the boy's dorm." Rachel spat back. But at that moment, she realized she needed to get out of there before someone noticed she had prolonged her stay after helping Spencer inside the building.

"Just wait a minute. Let me think." Rachel traced her lips with her fingertips.

"I just need to get some sleep. I'm headed home tomorrow." Spencer announced.

"Home?" Nate asked.

"Yeah. I'm gonna call my grandparents in the morning from the campus security office." Spencer's voice sounded hoarse and tired now. He needed sleep.

Rachel nodded once and did not add anything to the discussion. Instead, she thought about what that would mean for the rest of the group. With Spencer gone, there would be one less person in the circle exposed to the Ouija nightmare. At least, that's what she hoped.

"Nate, it's past 10:00 now. Just close the door. I've got to go. I'll see you guys tomorrow." Rachel chewed on her fingernails and moved toward the door.

"Damn it, man. Now nobody's gonna sleep tonight." Nate confessed. He stepped aside as Rachel reached for the door.

"I've got an exam in 4th period Chemistry tomorrow afternoon. I can't miss it, but meet me at the Chemistry Lab after class." Rachel had an idea.

"Okay." Nate agreed. "Where are we going?"

"The only place I know to turn. Amber and Stephanie are still playing the game. I can feel it."

Spencer shook his head.

Rachel gave him a puzzled look. "Why are you shaking your head, Spencer?"

"Amber and Stephanie aren't the only ones playing that game."

"What the hell? Who else is playing?" Nate's voice became loud.

"Shhh." Rachel put her index finger over her mouth and then pointed toward the wall, indicating the proximity of other people across the hall.

"You guys remember all those people over at the music building that night?"

"Yeah, and." Nate acknowledged.

"They've got their own board, man. I thought all this was bullshit until tonight."

Nate took a deep breath. "I'm scared as hell. I hate to admit it. But damn it, I'm scared, and I'm tired of this shit."

"I think we all are. Try to get some sleep. Oh, and I'll tell Josie to come." Rachel added.

"I hope she doesn't bring those other two with her." Nate had no desire to be around Amber or Stephanie. He agreed with Rachel and believed that they were summoning the spirit of Ryan Banks.

"Not happening. I'm outta here." Rachel didn't hesitate to agree with Nate. She was just as scared as he was, and she regretted exposing herself to the game. She opened the door and walked out leaving the two of them to fight sleep for the night.

She slipped through the door to the fire escape stairway and carefully descended down the stairs undetected by anyone else in the building. As she pushed the door open and rushed across the campus parking lot toward Kendall Hall, she thought about Josie and her relationship with Amber and Stephanie. And she wondered how deep her loyalty was with the two who refused to heed Officer Bobby's warning. If they were still stirring up the spirit at Kendall Hall, did Josie know about it? And if she did, was she still involved? How far would she go before she stopped playing a game with the dead? A game that had already proven to be a portal that allowed spirits to come forth into a dimension inhabited by the living. But the spirits weren't here for good. No, these spirits were here to cause harm. In any form or means possible. And even if it meant influencing a living soul to do its bidding. Even if it meant murder.

# Seventeen

The room was almost totally dark except for the candlelight that illuminated the faces of Amber Simons and Stephanie Baker. The candle's flame seemed to dance in rhythm as if it was under the influence of a magical conductor while Amber studied the board in front of her. Josie stood over them now seated in the center of the floor, the Ouija board positioned on their lap. Their knees touched, and their fingertips rested lightly on the planchette as it moved slowly in a circle around the board. Amber was taking the lead and serving as the medium, the same role she always assumed each time she contacted the dead. But tonight she started by only asking questions that required yes or no answers. She had become too enthralled by the spirit of Ryan Banks, talking to him nightly now even when Stephanie wasn't in the room. He had told her about important future dates in her life and who she could expect to meet. He had even predicted Spencer's accident, but she hadn't bothered to tell anyone.

Josie leaned against the wall and watched as the planchette seemed to snatch control right out of Amber's hands as it began to spell out a name.

R-A-C-H-E-L.

"Rachel?" Amber asked, a confused look on her face.

I-S.

"Yes? Rachel is?" Amber smiled. She gloated with creepy pride as she looked up at Josie.

C-O-M-I-N-G.

"Rachel is coming?" Amber was amazed. The spirit's ability to know future events before they happened was mesmerizing and addicting. She now felt a strange kinship to the spirit and refused to acknowledge any danger that Ryan Banks might bring.

*YES.*

"Oh shit. Is she coming to our room?" Amber asked.

*YES.*

"Ask it when?" Josie eagerly whispered.

Amber nodded. "When, Ryan? When is Rachel coming?"

N-O-W.

"Now?" Josie quickly moved away from the wall and started for the door when she was met with a cold burst of air that swirled around her. She gasped and stood dead still. Stephanie was freaked out and suddenly removed her fingers from the planchette.

"Wait. What are you doing?" Amber asked, annoyed by Stephanie's withdrawal.

Stephanie shook her head. "I got creeped out. This shit is too real sometimes."

"It's always real, Steph. Put your hands back on the board. It works better with two people." Amber's tone was demanding and acrimonious. She was becoming more easily angered each day that she continued her relationship with Ryan Banks.

Stephanie hesitated.

"Forget it, Stephanie. Rachel isn't coming. And even if she does, what's she going to do about it?"

"She thinks she is so beautiful. The way she flips her hair around. And she's constantly telling us what we should be doing." Amber bashed Rachel hard.

"Yep, she thinks she's so hot. Look, if she shows up, just tell her to go to hell." Josie chimed in, shrugging her shoulders as if Rachel meant nothing to her.

Stephanie nodded and placed her hands back on the board. Meanwhile, Rachel Thomas stood outside the door, her head bowed as tears pooled in her eyes, threatening to spill over at any second. She fought against the urge to cry and used her index finger to scoop away the moisture. Then she raised her fist in the air and slammed it against the door three times.

Josie let out a clipped scream and jerked her hands up to cover her mouth. In a simultaneous and swift response, Stephanie jumped up and flicked on the light.

"Oh my god. It's Rachel." Amber whispered as Stephanie slowly opened the door.

Rachel stood in the hall, her body rigid as she

observed the three of them with a cold, fixed stare. She said nothing and then slowly turned her eyes to meet Josie's.

"Hey, pretty girl. Where have you been?" Josie greeted Rachel in her usual sugary sweet tone, utterly indifferent to her own betrayal just seconds before, but Rachel now knew it was a fake friendship all along.

Rachel paused and glared at Josie with an all knowing smile while Josie stared back wide-eyed with a 'oh shit I'm caught' look.

"For the past three hours, I've been with Spencer at the hospital. He had an accident." Rachel spoke through pursed lips.

"Oh hell no. What happened? Is he okay?" Josie's tone changed to concern and an unspoken hope that Rachel had not overheard their venomous comments about her.

"He fell in his room. Just a freak accident. Fractured a rib, but he's okay now. Nate's staying with him tonight, but he says he's leaving campus tomorrow to stay with his grandmother." Rachel looked at Amber who attempted to hide the board with her body by leaning over it. Rachel frowned and took a long deep breath.

"Just so you all know. I came here to tell you that we're going to get help tomorrow after 4th period. But as I walked up to the door, I overheard you trashing me. And by the way, you can go to hell. All of you bitches."

Rachel turned and left them staring in disbelief as she walked back down the hall to her room. She shoved her key in the lock and pushed the door open then slammed it shut behind her.

The three of them stared at each other in guilty silence. Then Josie looked away and down at the floor. "I better get to bed. If I miss Biology one more time, I'm gonna get thrown out."

Stephanie glanced at Josie with a smirk on her face while Amber sat emotionless, her eyes fixed straight ahead. She didn't care what Rachel thought. She was so bewitched by the spirit of Ryan Banks that anyone who challenged her would be renounced without consideration.

Josie turned and reached for the door, but Amber stopped her. "Wait."

Josie looked back at Amber. "What?"

"I should have said something, but I guess I forgot. I think Ryan was trying to tell me that Spencer was going to have an accident." Amber said in a sheepish tone.

"Are you kidding me?" Stephanie piped up.

"Nope." Amber smiled, but her lips curved upward into a wicked grin.

Josie sighed heavily and dreaded having to face Rachel now, and she didn't want to hear anything else about the Ouija spirit. As she opened the door and walked out, she called out over her shoulder. "I'll catch you guys later."

Josie walked down the dimly lit hall toward her dorm room and wondered what she should say to Rachel. She felt remorse and wished that she had never been a participant in Amber's venomous backstabbing, but it was too late. And she had been caught. A willing contributor in the termination of a friendship. She stopped at the door and stood outside for a moment.

Then she turned the doorknob and tiptoed inside the dark room. The bathroom light illuminated a narrow path to the bunkbeds where Rachel was rolled on her right side and facing the wall.

Josie's joints popped as she walked across the room and climbed the ladder to reach the top bunk. The bed shook as she settled in causing Rachel to stir, but she turned over to the opposite side and fell fast asleep again.

Josie lay flat on her back and stared at the ceiling through the darkness. She listened to the absence of sound in the room, an eerie silence that encapsulated them both as they rested in their beds. She thought about the spirit in the board. *No one was safe anywhere because the spirit of Ryan Banks could travel.* He had none of the physical restraints that an earthly body imposed.

Josie struggled to banish her fearful thoughts. By thinking of Ryan Banks, she was unknowingly giving him power, and the spirit fed off of their fears. It empowered him, enabling him to be wherever the energy took him and at any time.

She closed her eyes and forced herself to imagine

sinking into a soft cocoon as she took long, deep breaths. She relaxed her shoulders and allowed her body to sink into the mattress. Within minutes, Josie was asleep, but not safe. She had granted an invitation to the spirit of Ryan Banks after placing herself in his presence each time her friend, Amber called him forth. She was an easy target, someone the spirit could easily attach to. She had little knowledge of the spirit world and little self-restraint. And the spirit of Ryan Banks needed her fear to grow more powerful.

The spirit swirled around the room, unseen and unfelt while the two young women slept. It's energy brushed through the air, leaving traces of icy cold spots scattered around the room. It peered at them through colorless, hollow eyes that were always invisible unless it was able to drain the life force out of an unsuspecting victim. But that had not happened in years. That had not happened since Margaret R. Banks had died in the river three miles away.

Josie stirred as the spirit inched closer to the bed. The bell on Rachel's dreamcatcher began to jingle as it vibrated against the wall. Then the sound of someone clicking their fingernails filled the air. The noises continued until Josie was lifted into a semi-sleeping state.

Josie tossed and turned until all at once, she heard the distinct sound of a wild animal's panting. It slithered closer and closer to her face until she felt its hot, moist breath against her skin. And then like a shot out of nowhere, Josie's eyes flew open as she felt a fierce and powerful force push against her shoulders, shoving her deeper into the mattress until she gasped for air.

She tried to scream, but she couldn't move. Her eyes darted from side to side, wild with fright and searching for her attacker, but she saw nothing. Her attacker had no physical face or body, only a supernatural force that was hell bent on smothering the life out of her.

She pushed up hard and fast, trying to free herself from its grip until she was finally able to find her voice. She screamed with all of her might. A blood curdling scream that echoed beyond the dorm room's walls and into the hall.

Rachel leaped out of the bed, shaking from head to toe. "What the hell is going on?!" She yelled.

Lights came on across the hall and in their suite

mate's room as the neighbors heard Josie's screams. Directly below them on the first floor, the dorm mother quickly threw on a robe and raced up the stairs to the second floor. Within seconds, she was standing in the second floor hall.

"Girls, open this door." Ms. Ruth yelled as her fist pounded against the door.

Rachel raced to the door and flung it open as Josie wailed in long, hysteric sobs.

Rachel then rushed to her side and tried to console her. "Josie, it's okay. It's gone now."

Josie shook her head and screamed. "No, it tried to kill me! Ryan Banks tried to kill me!"

Ms. Ruth stepped inside. She looked around the room as if she was searching for someone to appear. She then looked back at Rachel.

"Who is Ryan Banks?"

Rachel hesitated. She wondered how the hell she was going to explain a Ouija spirit named Ryan Banks to the seventy-year old dorm mother. Ms. Ruth studied her with folded arms that partially concealed her sagging breasts now visible through the robe's thin fabric and her absence of a bra.

"She was just having a bad dream, Ms. Ruth. She's okay now." Rachel stated a half-truth, but it was a necessary cover-up.

Josie shook her head but declined to offer any other explanation. She continued to sob.

"I'm sorry you had a bad dream, Josie. That was quite a scare." Ms. Ruth turned to walk out, and then stopped. "Say, have you girls been moving furniture again after 8:00? You know, I told you to stop that."

Rachel looked at Josie. "No, we haven't. I don't know what you're talking about. We don't really have any furniture to move." She pointed to the beds and scanned the room.

"Okay, well—Like I told you before, I can hear everything that goes on up here from my apartment underneath your room. You girls try to get some sleep now." Ms. Ruth walked out into the hall, leaving the door slightly ajar. Rachel overheard her ordering the other girls back to bed after she told them that everything was alright.

Josie looked at Rachel through blood shot eyes. Her

lips trembled as she mumbled, and tears spilled down her cheeks. "Don't turn out the lights. If I have to stay here the rest of the damn night, I want the lights on."

"Don't worry. There's no way in hell that I'm turning the lights off now. No way in hell." Rachel promised as she sat down on the edge of the bed and prayed.

# *Eighteen*

At daylight, Rachel awakened to excruciating stomach pain that felt like needles puncturing her insides. She moaned and rubbed her abdomen before rolling off the bed and into the floor. The humming of the overhead fluorescent light reminded her that they had left the lights on all night, and she rolled her eyes up to see Josie still sleeping in the overhead bunk. She bent forward and slowly slid her feet across the floor until she reached the vanity sink. She turned on the valves and splashed warm water across her face then reached for a bottle of Advil and tossed two into her mouth.

Just as she swallowed the pills, she caught a glimpse of Josie's image from the mirror in front of her as she was climbing down the bunkbed ladder. Rachel turned to greet her, but just as she opened her mouth to speak she found herself speechless as she stared at nothingness. Bewildered and afraid, her mouth fell open as she viewed Josie still lying flat on her back in the bed. Rachel's skin tingled from head to toe, and she called out with urgency.

"Josie! Josie, wake up!" She walked over to the side of the bed and noticed the dark circles under Josie's eyes. She reached out to touch Josie and lightly pushed against her shoulder.

"Josie!" Rachel shouted this time, determined to get a response from the sleeping dead.

Josie grunted and opened one eye.

Rachel stood in front of her, still holding her stomach. "We need to get going."

Josie rolled over and threw her legs over the side of the bed letting them dangle. She rubbed her eyes and sighed. "God, I feel like hell."

Rachel ignored her comment and began to get dressed while continuing to rub her abdomen.

"Are you alright?" Josie noticed Rachel's painful posture.

"Yeah, my stomach is hurting. Must be a virus or something." She replied.

Josie looked down at her hands and picked at her fingernails while contemplating her next words to Rachel. She hesitated for a few moments, quietly chewing on her thumbnail, and then she looked across the room where Rachel was now twisting her hair into a ponytail.

"Hey-- I'm really sorry about last night. I was a piece of shit."

Rachel's face dropped, and she looked up at Josie with grieving eyes. She nodded once. "Okay."

"No, I really mean it. I don't want to lose your friendship." Josie's eyes watered.

Rachel stopped fooling with her hair and focused on Josie. "That really hurt, you know. Why did you say it? If you didn't mean it, why did you agree with Amber?"

"I don't know. Maybe I'm just a little jealous, but I'm sorry. I want to be friends."

Rachel huffed. "Jealous of what? Seriously?" She

shook her head. Rachel paused as Josie stepped forward and reached out to hug her.

Rachel teared up as she allowed Josie to embrace her.

For a moment, the energy in the room changed, and Rachel noticed it getting lighter. A tear rolled down her cheek. She was mentally and physically exhausted from weeks of worry, sleeplessness, and the demands of college studies. She reasoned that it had finally caught up with her as her stomach churned and stabbing pains overwhelmed her.

"Josie, something's bad wrong. I'm sick, Spencer had a terrible accident, and now all of us are seeing things and hearing things we can't explain. And these damn dreams. These damn dreams are driving us crazy!"

"Yeah, this is screwed up as hell. I used to not even believe in this shit." Josie sighed and wiped her eyes, smearing mascara across her cheek.

"I think this thing is after all of us, and none of it makes sense. Do you realize that we can't tell anybody about this? We have nowhere to turn." Rachel closed her eyes and massaged her temples. She desperately wanted to make sense of what was happening to all of them or better yet, she wanted someone to tell her that it was all a bad dream. She just wanted it to end.

"I know." Josie whispered in agreement.

"Right before you got up a few minutes ago, I was washing my face at the sink, and I saw you in the mirror. You were climbing down the ladder, but when I turned around, you were flat on your back in the bed. How the hell do you explain that?"

Josie stared at Rachel with shock and disbelief. "I've seen the same thing. Except I thought it was you."

"There's no way in hell that we can be imagining what's happening to us. Me, you, Nate, and now Spencer have all had some sort of freaky encounter with this thing." Rachel was exasperated.

"Spencer? What happened to him?"

"Last night. I told you." Rachel said.

"No, you told us that Spencer had an accident. You didn't say anything about the spirit."

Rachel nodded once. "Okay, well—Spencer said that it spoke to him. He heard its voice, Josie."

"Jesus Christ. What did it say?"

"It told him to kill of us." Rachel whispered.

"Oh hell no!" Josie was horrified.

"Nate and I are going to see someone this afternoon after my 4th period class. Someone who might be able to help."

"Who? How did you find them?" Josie asked in the form of an urgent demand.

"I don't have time to go into it. We've got class in 15 minutes, but meet me at the Chemistry Lab later."

"Okay, definitely. I'll be there."

Rachel picked up her backpack and slung it over her shoulder then turned and held up her finger, motioning for Josie to pay attention.

"As much as I think Amber and Stephanie need to go with us today, they're not invited."

Josie expressed a mirthless smile. "They wouldn't go anyway." Rachel returned the same expression and walked out the door.

Six hours later.

Josie and Nate stood outside the Chemistry Building

where they waited on Rachel as she finished the last two questions on her exam. Inside the classroom, she struggled to stay focused as she battled an occasional twinge of stomach pain and her body's desire to sleep. Finally, she colored in the oval next to "A" on the answer key. She then quickly shoved her pencil into her backpack and walked to the front of the room where she turned in her test sheet.

As she walked toward the exit door, she saw Nate and Josie through the window. She pushed the door open and wasted no time as she motioned for them to get in the car. Rachel got in the driver's seat and shut the door with a bang.

"Where exactly are we going?" Nate quizzed Rachel in his usual detective's tone. He gazed at Rachel in the rearview mirror, noticing distress in her eyes, but once again he found himself studying the shape of her face, the soft creaminess of her skin, and the way she could never hide what she was really feeling. Like any good artist, he noticed everything. And Rachel had become his favorite study.

She waited to answer him and instead put the key in

the ignition and started the car. As she pulled the gear shift down to reverse and backed out of the parking lot, she turned to the backseat and looked at Nate.

"Saint Thomas Catholic Church." Rachel slid the gear shift to drive and pushed hard against the gas pedal as the car sped forward. Within seconds, she was turning the corner onto the main highway and headed toward the office of Sister Elizabeth Williams. She didn't give anyone a chance to object as she focused her eyes straight ahead. If Ryan Banks was *what*, not *who* she thought he was, she knew they needed a kind of help that couldn't be found anywhere else.

# Nineteen

Rachel drove a couple miles east of Riverside College and stopped at a small, red brick church. She parked her car at the rear of the building. A light shone through an outside door window that led to the basement apartment where Sister Elizabeth Williams lived.

"Looks like she's home." Rachel eyed the tall, stained glass windows at the side of the church.

"Who is *she*?" Josie asked.

"Sister Williams. She's the nun who lives here."

"You know her?" Nate asked nervously.

"Of course not. But I know that she's lived here for

years. She ministers to people in the community. You know, like a preacher does." Rachel looked at Nate in the rearview mirror.

Rachel turned the ignition off and then glanced over at Josie who was steadily popping her knuckles. Josie's mind reeled with 'what ifs'. Her anxiety grew minute by minute, and she dreaded getting out of the car. She had no idea what to expect from their meeting with a Catholic nun. This wasn't your typical 'go to Sunday church' meeting. This was a request for help from paranormal experiences brought on by a Ouija spirit. *How were they going to explain that to a nun?*

"Halleluiah!" Nate slapped the back of the seat causing Rachel and Josie to jump. Rachel gasped and covered her eyes with her hands.

"Damn, Nate. Don't be an ass." Josie yelled.

Nate chuckled. "Awe. Relax."

"Are you?" Rachel turned to look at him now leaned forward, resting his arms across the back of the seat.

"Relaxed?" He asked.

"Yeah." Rachel shook her head, annoyed and scared all at the same time.

"Hell, no." Nate responded with a nervous laugh.

"Are we going to see the priest?" Josie asked.

"Nah, I don't think the priest is here all the time." Rachel guessed.

"Let's go." Rachel ceased any more questions and got out of the car, leaving Nate and Josie to follow.

She walked up a narrow ramp and knocked on the heavy wood door. Within a few seconds, the three of them heard someone from inside the apartment shuffling around.

A loud click sounded from the other side of the door as Sister Elizabeth Williams slowly turned the locks and pulled the door open just enough to peer out and see Rachel's face.

"Yes, can I help you?" The eighty-year old nun asked. Her voice was soft, yet feeble and characteristic of her age.

She held the door close to her body, refusing to open the door wide enough for them to enter. Rachel turned her eyes downward, trying not to stare at the nun's small, short stature clothed in a black habit. Her gray hair was finely combed and pulled tight in a bun at the base of her neck, and her eyes drooped with crow's feet that traced down her cheeks, turning into deep set wrinkles. Wrinkles that housed the memories of every path she had followed for Christ.

Rachel finally spoke. "Yes, may we speak with you? We need help, Sister."

The nun nodded and held up her index finger. "Go around to the front of the church and wait. I'll open the door."

"Thank you." Rachel looked at the nun with humbled eyes and answered in a deeply appreciative tone.

The group turned and went around to the front of the building where they waited. After a moment, the nun returned with her head now covered by a veil. She pulled the front door to the sanctuary open and invited the three of them inside. She then turned and made the sign of the cross, the ancient Catholic gesture that invokes the Holy Trinity before she motioned for them to follow her to the front of the church. She then offered them a seat in the pew closest to the altar while she sat down in a folding chair facing them.

The elderly nun sat quiet as she stared into the eyes of each person sitting before her. Josie fidgeted, prompting Nate to speak up and introduce the three of them.

"Sister, my name is Nate Larson. This is my friends, Rachel Thomas and Josie Norton."

Sister Elizabeth nodded and smiled, her hands clasped together and resting in her lap. "I'm Sister Elizabeth Williams. What's troubling you today?"

Rachel took a deep breath before she spoke. "Something is happening to us. Something we can't explain."

"What do you mean?" Sister Elizabeth didn't sound surprised.

Rachel hesitated and looked at Nate. Her heart beat faster. "Sister, we used a Ouija board a few weeks ago, and ever since then—

"Do you know what you've done?" Sister Williams interrupted. This wasn't the first time that college students had knocked on her door. Many had sought help after hours and late at night when they should have been sleeping.

Rachel's mouth fell open, and tears began to flood her eyes. She slowly nodded and then waited for the severe tongue lashing that she was certain was forthcoming as the old nun raised her index finger in the air and moved it from side to side.

Nate watched as Rachel turned her eyes away from what she assumed was condemnation. He placed a hand around Rachel's shoulders and held his palm up, indicating for Sister Williams to be gentle.

"Sister Williams, none of us believed the board could really connect with the dead. It's just a game." He explained.

Sister Williams dropped her finger and slowly closed her eyes with a simple nod. She offered a smile of understanding and then opened her eyes. Rachel quietly observed the nun's reaction and was glad that her mood and tone was nothing like she had just feared.

"That's what they all think. How many times has my door been opened to kids just like yourselves? All of you are students at Riverside? Is that right?" Sister Williams was kind and respectful, but her deliverance was parental as she considered what the three of them had unleashed.

Josie interjected. "Yes, Ma'am." Josie then looked at Nate, taking full responsibility for what was happening.

"Hey-- All this is really my fault. I introduced Rachel to Amber and Stephanie."

"Shhh." Rachel put her finger over her mouth. "It's too late for that, and there's no need for you to feel that way. We were all a part of it. Right now, we just need some answers." Rachel turned back to Sister Williams.

"Two girls on campus are still playing the board, and they're playing it in our dorm. They've even become friends with a spirit named Ryan Banks who has told them all kinds of things."

Sister Williams's skin grew pale. She mumbled to herself. "Margaret Banks."

Rachel vaguely heard the name as it escaped from the nun's lips. "What did you say? Did you say Margaret Banks?"

Sister Williams ignored Rachel's question and continued with stern instructions. "You must not play with that game anymore. Do you hear what I am saying? You're opening a door for bad spirits to come through."

"Sister, I heard you say 'Margaret Banks'. Who is Margaret Banks?" Rachel pressed.

Nate and Josie looked at each other in confusion. "Yeah, who is Margaret Banks?" Nate asked.

Rachel had not told anyone about the obituary she found at the library. Rachel glanced at Nate and Josie and whispered.

"That's what I've mean wanting to tell you guys. I found the obituary in the—

Rachel didn't finish her sentence. She turned her attention to Sister Elizabeth Williams instead and didn't utter another sound as she waited for her response.

Sister Williams breathed deep as she studied the three of them through narrowed eyes. She massaged her hands in an attempt to calm her growing concern for their safety. Then in a solemn and foreboding tone, she began to reveal the true identity of Ryan Banks.

"Margaret Ryan Banks was a beautiful young teacher at Riverside many years ago, and as anyone would expect, she accumulated a number of secret admirers among her students. She never had any trouble out of anybody even though many of the young men flirted with her. But a few months before she died, one of her students took an exceptional liking to her. He followed her everywhere. Sometimes showing up outside her class at the end of the day. A week before she died, she told one of the police officers at Riverside that the kid was stalking her."

She paused and looked away, her eyes began to moisten. She remembered the news of Margaret's death and the impact it had on the church. Margaret was one of their most beloved members and a one year old newlywed in the church's congregation.

"And then one morning—

Sister Williams paused and looked down at her hands, clasping them tighter before she continued.

"One morning they found her car in the river. When they pulled her body out of the car, the officer saw the bruises across her neck. And the impressions of his fingers where he had strangled her..." Her voice trailed off.

Chills covered all of their bodies as they listened in horror. "Ryan Banks was never a man." Rachel whispered.

"But who is the spirit? And why is it pretending to be a male ghost? He even told us that he committed suicide after being dumped by his girlfriend." Josie's voice trembled.

"No one was ever arrested for Margaret's murder. But the rumors circulated around the campus. Before the boy could be questioned, he killed himself."

"God help us." Rachel prayed aloud.

"Listen to me." Sister Williams issued a grave warning. "You must do what I tell you. It's been a long time, but there have been others who have come to my door, and we prayed that those spirits would be silenced." The nun stood up from her chair and hobbled over to a hidden closet near the altar. She removed a small vile of holy water and handed it to Nate.

"When you return to your rooms, take this holy water and dip your fingers into it as you recite this prayer. Make the sign of the cross as you say the prayer aloud." She handed Nate a scroll of paper with a sacred blessing typed in small print.

"Bless each corner of your room and bless yourself. You have opened a portal for the Devil, and you must not play that game anymore. Do you understand?" Sister Williams was stern and unrelenting.

Josie's hands were shaking as she received a vile of holy water from Sister Williams. "Ma'am, two of my friends are still playing the board."

Sister Williams shook her head. "Stay away. Your friends are in danger."

"But they think the Ouija board is just a game." Josie stated as a matter of fact.

Sister Williams reached for Josie's hand. She wrapped her cold frail fingers tight around Josie's palm. She leaned closer, her pale blue eyes searching the scared soul of Josie Norton, and then she spoke. With conviction and certainty, she named the portal that had unleashed evil at Riverside.

"It's not a game, my dear. It's the Devil's board."

# Twenty

Rachel slammed the car door shut. Her hands were trembling as she pushed the key into the ignition and started the car. She hurriedly shifted it into reverse and then pulled out of the church parking lot. She glanced in the rearview mirror as if she was expecting to see Sister Williams standing at the door watching them leave. She breathed deep as the car sped forward and wiped a bead of sweat from her brow. No one said a word until one mile later, Josie broke the silence.

"We have to tell Amber and Stephanie. I'm scared as hell. What if that thing can possess somebody?"

Rachel turned her head and looked at Josie. "What if it already has?"

"Oh, Hell!" Nate shuddered.

"Amber is obsessed with that board. I don't think she'll listen to us." Rachel argued.

"But we have to try. I know she's planning to use the board again tonight. It's the night before Halloween. Do you know what that means?"

Rachel shrugged her shoulders and raised her eyebrows with a dumb look.

It's called The Devil's Night." Josie affirmed.

Rachel hit the brakes, throwing everyone forward. She yelled and threw her hands in the air.

"What the hell? We've got a nun who just told us that we've been playing the Devil's board and now you're telling us that Amber is going to use that damn thing again on the Devil's night? We are totally fucked, people." Her voice continued to escalate, almost screaming.

"Calm down, will ya?" Nate pleaded. "I almost busted my damn teeth against the seat."

Josie jerked around and looked at Nate rubbing his

mouth as if he was expecting a bloody lip. She then turned back around and stared at the road in front of them as Rachel pressed the accelerator of the car and drove toward the college entrance.

"Just relax, Rachel. I'll tell them. We just need to bless our dorm room and do what Sister Williams told us." Josie took responsibility for her friends and promised to warn them.

A sudden piercing pain shot through Rachel's abdomen again causing her to jerk. She grimaced and gripped the steering wheel tight as she slowly brought the car to a stop outside Kendall Hall.

"What's wrong?" Nate leaned forward and touched Rachel's shoulder.

Rachel shook her head and tried to answer, but the pains continued to come with increasing intensity. She took several slow breaths and then finally responded. "It's stomach pains. Not sure what the hell is causing it."

"Can I do anything to help?" Nate looked at Rachel with the genuine concern of a love-struck guy. He wanted to stay with her but knew that was impossible.

Rachel shook her head. "I'm okay. I just need to go

home until all this Ouija shit stops."

"Josie, do you know where Amber is now?" Nate asked.

"No, I haven't seen her today."

"Well, I don't want to be in Kendall Hall when she starts playing that board tonight." Rachel declared as she massaged her abdomen.

"Me either." Josie agreed.

"Let's get some dinner later at the cafeteria, and we can decide what we're doing then. Meanwhile, I think I'll drink this holy water that the good sister gave me." Nate joked.

Rachel responded with a mocking laugh and rolled her eyes. "You might need to."

As Nate got out of the car, Rachel waved goodbye and felt an overwhelming sense of dread wash over her. It was dread unlike anything she had ever felt before and it consumed her, enveloping her body as visions flashed through her mind. A horrid premonition of what was to come in less than four hours.

Dusk had descended over Riverside campus as Rachel and Josie napped in their bunkbeds. Rachel had set the alarm for 5:30 p.m. so that the two of them could meet Nate at the cafeteria for dinner, but before the alarm could sound, Rachel rolled over and opened her eyes. The room was almost dark. She fumbled around the bedside table, searching for the shut-off button on the alarm clock. She then swung her legs over the side of the bed and stood up before walking to the opposite side of the room where she flicked on the lights.

Meanwhile at the other end of the hall, Amber Simmons had entered her dorm room and without any forethought or sense of caution, she unpacked the Ouija board, sat down in the center of the floor, and placed the board on her lap. Within seconds, the spirit had been brought to life, and the planchette raced back and forth.

But tonight was different. Tonight, Amber had decided that she wanted Ryan Banks to prove he was real. She wanted a sign, and she wasn't accepting anything less than a dramatic display of his presence. And so she taunted him. Pressuring the spirit to come forth and do something that could only be done through supernatural means.

"Ryan, are you real? Some people don't believe me when I tell them that you are real."

*YES.*

"I don't believe you, Ryan." Amber teased, playing a power game with the entity that she was destined to lose.

The planchette sped up; it raced faster from side to side.

"Do you want to show me who you are?"

The planchette darted to the upper left corner.

*YES.*

"How?" Amber coaxed.

And then it began to spell words, snatching control out of Amber's hands.

K-I-L-L Y-O-U.

Amber gasped and shivered as the temperature in the room dropped. She struggled to maintain control of the planchette as her fingers became like icicles. A few seconds passed while she sat still, her hands hovering over the board. Then determined not to be outdone, Amber Simmons continued her treacherous game alone with Ryan Banks.

"You can't kill anybody, Ryan." Amber showed a false sense of bravery.

I.

C-A-N.

"Prove it, Ryan. Prove it!" She shouted, taunting the spirit until all at once the board lifted off her legs and flew through the air. Amber screamed and jumped up.

She darted toward the door as the desk chair suddenly slid across the floor toward her, barely missing her legs. She flung the door open and let out another terrifying scream as massive pillows of black smoke swirled into the room.

A fierce wave of heat slapped her in the face causing her to gasp and fall backwards onto the floor. She coughed and gagged unable to see in front of her as she scrambled around with her hands stretched out in front of her until she was finally able to crawl through the doorway.

Screams echoed down the hall as girls raced from their dorm rooms searching for an escape route, but the entry to the fire escape was completely blocked by a mountainous black cloud that was fast consuming the entire building.

Rachel heard the horrific screams just as she reached for the light switch. She flicked on the switch and flung the door open. The smell of sulfur immediately caused her to choke as smoke invaded the room.

"Josie, get up! Fire! Fire!" Rachel screamed with all her strength, straining her voice.

Josie panicked, flinging her arms in the air as she rolled off the bed and hit the floor. She screamed out in pain as her kneecap busted against the hard tile floor.

"Rachel, wait! I can't walk!" Josie yelled. She cried and grabbed her knee.

Rachel stopped, her body still bent over to avoid the heat and smoke that was rising fast, smothering the breath out of her. She reached out, offering Josie her arm.

"Oh, God, Josie, you've got to try. Come on. Take my arm and drag your leg." Josie reached for the bunkbed ladder and pulled herself up. She then turned and grabbed onto Rachel, sliding her leg across the floor.

Rachel heard the sound of sirens in the distance as she held onto the side of the wall and scooted forward. Her eyes burned, forcing them to squint almost shut as she felt her way to the stairway, her arms extended in front of her like the blind.

Finally in what seemed like hours but was actually within seconds, Josie and Rachel reached the stairway and made their way out of the building as others raced past them on the stairs, still screaming in horror.

Rachel opened her eyes wide just as her feet touched the first floor. She looked straight ahead where emergency personnel were now rushing inside the lobby entrance. Firefighters pushed past them and raced up the stairs. And then a familiar face appeared in the doorway.

There staring her in the face was Officer Bobby Edwards. He carefully pushed past a stampede of scared females exiting the building. He hurried to Josie's side and placed his arms around her shoulders, offering support as he helped her through the front door while Rachel coughed and spit, struggling to catch her breath.

"My knee. My knee is screwed up." Josie cried.

"It'll be okay, Josie. You probably just tore some ligaments, but don't worry. An ambulance is on the way." Bobby tried to ease Josie's fear, but wasn't much help as she clenched her teeth in agony. He then turned and dashed back into the lobby.

Rachel sat down on the sidewalk next to Josie. "It was the board. I know it. Amber was using the damn board." Josie said through sobs.

Rachel let out a giant sigh and wept.

Just then, Amber Simmons ran out the front door of Kendall Hall. Officer Bobby was behind her.

"Rachel, don't." Josie saw fire come into Rachel's eyes as she watched Amber Simmons walk past. She knew Rachel wanted to beat the living hell out of her.

Officer Bobby stopped at Josie's feet. He watched Amber walk past them. "Do you know who set the fire in the building?"

Josie looked at Rachel.

"Someone set a fire? It wasn't an accident?" Josie asked, not surprised.

"I don't think so." He looked over at Amber Simmons who stared at the building with an emotionless expression. Her face void of compassion or concern for anyone else's well-being.

Josie looked up at the officer. "Amber Simmons was using the board. She told me that she was going to make the spirit prove that he was real tonight since it's the Devil's night. The night before Halloween. She said she was going to make it give her a sign."

Officer Bobby's face fell into a look of rage.

"Which room is hers?" There was no disputing the anger in his voice.

"At that end of the hall. On the right." Rachel pointed to the right end of the building.

Bobby darted through the front door and up the stairs. Firefighters sprayed water against the inside wall of Room 219, saturating the hot melted pieces of a stereo that had mysteriously burst into flames after hours of being left on.

Across the hall, Bobby hastily entered Amber's room where he found the Ouija board still laying in the floor just inside the door. He reached down and grabbed the board then ran back downstairs and through the lobby doors. As he bolted outside with the board in hand, Amber marched toward him, demanding that he return it to her.

"This is what you want?" Officer Bobby asked in a tone that sent a clear message to back away.

"Yeah, it's mine. Give it back." Amber stepped forward.

Rachel stood up. She moved to Officer Bobby's side. "That bullshit board game has caused a lot of trouble around here." Rachel confronted her.

Officer Bobby ignored Amber's vindictive stare and walked past her to the edge of the building. He reached in his pocket and pulled out the cigarette lighter tucked inside a pack of Marlboros that he had just bought. He then took the board and with a loud crack, he slammed the board against his knee splitting it in half. He shoved the splintered pieces into a round metal trashcan. Then he bent down and picked up a handful of pine straw, tossing it on top of the board. He flicked the lighter three times, exposing a glowing yellow flame.

"Stop!" Amber screamed, but it was too late. Bobby lit the straw. The flames quickly engulfed the board, shriveling the straw to ashes.

Just then Nate came around the side of the building and ran to Rachel's side. Dozens of other students and onlookers had now gathered around the scene.

"Are you guys alright? What's going on?" Nate was almost breathless, worried and yet relieved to see that Rachel and Josie were not hurt. He looked at Amber across the lawn now staring at them. Her eyes seemed to grow more wicked as the flames climbed higher.

Rachel didn't answer and ignored Amber's stare. She pointed to the fire whose flames now glowed and danced in the darkness.

"Rachel?" Nate studied her. She was mesmerized by the fiery show, ignoring everyone around her. "Hey—

He paused, but couldn't take his eyes off of her. And then he touched her arm. "Rachel? What the hell just happened over here?"

Finally, Rachel turned her head in his direction and

acknowledged him. "I'm watching it burn."

"Watching what burn?" Nate looked puzzled. The flames blew heat closer toward him.

Rachel slowly rolled her eyes away from the blaze and returned Amber's sadistic glare, daring Amber with a silent threat and a promise of trouble if she made the wrong move. Then she turned to Nate, and mumbled softly.

"The Devil's Board."

# GOOD BYE.

# *Epilogue*

By morning, word of the fire in Kendall Hall had spread around Riverside campus.    Dozens of curious students tried to sneak past the taped off areas to get a glimpse of the room where the demon had started the fire, but eventually the chaos calmed.  By the end of the semester, the second floor of Kendall Hall had been cleaned and the walls repainted for its next college bound tenants.

Within days of the incident, Rachel Thomas moved back home.  Soon after, she was hospitalized with an undisclosed illness that caused flu-like symptoms such as severe abdominal pain, weight loss, and fatigue.  Within a year of leaving Riverside, she had fully recovered and enrolled at another nearby college.  Stephanie Baker remained a student at Riverside for the next two years. She never spoke of the Ouija incident again.

Amber Simmons reportedly packed the last remaining items she could salvage from her dorm room and loaded them into her 1979 Volkswagen Rabbit before dropping out of Riverside College. She then left the campus and traveled to California to join her mother who was vacationing near Malibu Beach. She was never seen or heard from again.

Josie Norton finished another semester of college, but later dropped out after failing most of her classes and losing her financial aid. She later got married and started a family. Spencer Gordon never returned to Riverside.

Nate Larson completed a two year program at Riverside and transferred to a senior university where he completed an undergrad degree in Graphic Design. His experience with the Ouija board caused months of suffering as he battled nightmarish visions each time he recalled his time at Riverside. Neither he nor Rachel Thomas ever played with *The Devil's Board* again.

# Before you play *The Devil's Board...*
## <u>OUIJA Tips & Rules</u>

*Never use the Ouija Board alone!

*Never use the Ouija Board if you are sick or emotionally unbalanced and suffering from depression, excessive stress, or other emotional issues. This can make you vulnerable to possession.

*If you suspect that you are under spiritual attack, meet with a member of the clergy who can pray with you.

*Never let the spirit have control of the board.

*If the planchette goes to the four corners of the board, it might be a malevolent spirit who is attempting to attach itself to you!

*In the event that the planchette moves repeatedly in a figure eight pattern, it suggests that an evil soul is in control of the board.

*Always say GOODBYE or the evil spirits will remain behind to haunt the operator.

*The spirit of the Ouija sometimes appears overly friendly and accommodating to the user. It creates "wins" causing the user to become increasingly dependent on the board. This is called Progressive Entrapment and can lead to demon possession.

*Evil spirits contacted through the Ouija board will endeavor to win your confidence with flattery and a show of supernatural abilities such as foretelling the future.

*Always be observant and never upset the spirits by taunting them or asking them to prove that they are real.

*Never use the Ouija in a graveyard or place where a terrible death has occurred or you will bring forth malevolent entities.

*Sometimes an evil spirt can inhabit a board. When this happens, no other spirits will be able to use it.

*There is only one proper way to dispose of the Ouija board. Break the board into seven pieces, sprinkle it with Holy Water, and then bury it.

*NEVER leave the planchette on the board if you aren't using it.

*Three things NEVER to ask a Ouija board: Never ask about God, Never ask when you are going to die, and...

**NEVER, NEVER, NEVER, ask it to show itself!**

Have you heard about this story?
A #1 Bestseller!

## **Inspired by True Events**

On December 21, 1974, Liz Bradford was murdered in the front parking lot of the prestigious Rex Plaza located in Elvis Presley's hometown of Tupelo, Mississippi. Her husband, Devon Bradford was also involved in the shooting and transported to North Mississippi Medical Center where he underwent surgery and first crossed Natalie Houston's path. She was his operating room nurse and had no idea that within three years she would be married to a killer. Haunted by the ghost of Liz Bradford, Natalie becomes the target of paranormal activity and a string of coincidences that will ultimately paint a picture of what's coming for her. Inspired by a true story, The Haunting of Natalie Bradford is the incredible tale of how Natalie Bradford finds herself entangled in a series of prophetic coincidences that foretells her future and reveals her lover's guilt. Prophecy is all around us, but are we paying attention to the messages we are receiving? Denial can be deadly. Are you next?

*The Haunting of Natalie Bradford is available as*

*Hardback, Paperback, and EBook.*

## *Do YOU Believe?*

A story inspired by the real life Mississippi Mystic, Seymour Prater. Known throughout the South for his mysterious and miraculous abilities, he could "see" beyond the barriers of time and space while identifying a man's killer, finding stolen objects, and even locating lost people. Seymour Prater left behind a supernatural legacy and one unsolved murder that terrified a Mississippi town as the community battled their fears of the living and a dead man's ghost that haunted the 'Old Floyd Place'.

CPSIA information can be obtained
at www.ICGtesting.com
Printed in the USA
FSHW010756171218
54527FS